and O

"Ms. Chase cer   ....u a short
story."
    Long and Short Reviews

"Ms. Chase offers an ending that was a complete surprise."
    Single Titles

"I love the dark edged (this term is used so I don't scare off readers who shy away from 'horror') themes."
    I Smell Sheep

"With this...Gini Koch - this time writing as Jemma Chase - explores another style of writing than her usual snark and wit and proves she doesn't need them to keep this reader interested."
    Pearls Cast Before a McPig

The Disciple
and Other Stories of the Paranormal

By Gini Koch
Writing as
Jemma Chase

The Disciple and Other Stories of the Paranormal
Published by Jemma Chase at CreateSpace

The Disciple first published by Musa Publishing November 2011
Hotter Than Hell first published by Musa Publishing October 2011
Strange Protection first published by Penumbra eMagazine Volume 1, Issue 3, December 2011

Editors: Mary Fiore
Cover Artist: Lisa Dovichi

ISBN: 978-1-50865-3653

Jemma Chase
http://www.ginikoch.com

Dedication

To my husband, the man who puts up with my proclivities, bizarre cravings, fascination with the weird, and need for constant heat even when it's warm out.

Acknowledgments

Thanks and love to my wonderful agent, Cherry Weiner, and my also wonderful critique partner, Lisa Dovichi. Thanks again to all the good folks at Artichoke Head and everyone on Team Gini – couldn't have gotten this done without all of you!

And many thanks to my family for constant, loving support and lots and lots of red wine (hey, it's the closest thing to blood I can legally find) and chocolate.

Table of Contents

STRANGE PROTECTION

She was finally able to stop running for a few moments.

She took advantage of the near wall shrouded in darkness, leaned against it, and tried not to pant out loud.

The place seemed deserted; then she noticed the man standing just outside of the small circles of light coming from the train station's few lamps. He was dressed like a typical businessman — suit, heavy overcoat, gloves, bulky briefcase. She wondered for a moment why he was taking such a late train into the city, then froze, examining him carefully, in case he was one of them.

He was clean-shaven, his hair carefully trimmed and arranged. His clothes looked to be of good quality, but that was all she could discern. He didn't seem to be doing anything other than waiting. That probably meant he wasn't with them, was just here, waiting to go home.

She knew she had at least ten minutes before the train arrived, maybe more. She also knew she couldn't stay in the open the entire time or they would find her. They'd assume she'd run here to escape, and she didn't want to be a sitting duck.

He'd noticed her before she'd reached the station, but had chosen not to react. He watched her out of the corner of his eye instead. She seemed like a frightened animal and he wondered what had happened to her. He assumed he knew, but then, he'd been mistaken once or twice before, in the past.

She moved out of the shadows, and now he could see she wasn't wearing any shoes. He wondered if she'd kicked them off in her flight from whatever had her terrified, or if they were in the backpack she wore.

She tried to walk normally but he detected a slight limp. As she got closer, he could tell the dress she wore was extremely thin, not at all appropriate for the weather. He figured she'd had a coat but abandoned it somewhere along the way.

Her hair was tousled, her breath still unsteady, her face slightly streaked with dirt, her eyes wild. But she managed to give him a cavalier smile as she got nearer.

"Car broke down," she said briefly. "Hope the train gets here soon."

He nodded. "Give it about fifteen minutes. It runs late on the last trip."

She grimaced. "Well, it'll give me time to freshen up." She laughed, nodded to him, and walked into the restroom behind them.

He looked where she'd been standing. There was a slight smudge there. Blood. He could tell even from a distance. He was never wrong, not about blood.

She managed to clean the cut on her foot somewhat. Putting her shoes on hurt, but she had nowhere left to run now, and trying to get onto the train barefoot might cause too many questions.

Questions meant delays, and she had no time for delays.

She washed her face and made sure that the proof was safe in her backpack. She brushed her hair quickly and took the time to tie it back with a scrunchie. She started to sling her pack back on, then reconsidered.

She opened it up again and took out one of the pictures and a pen. She wrote her name, the date, and what was truly in the picture on the back. She gave the address of the house, and instructions to enter armed with silver bullets. Then she slid the picture up into the paper towel dispenser, far enough that it wouldn't come out right away. It was the best she could do, and while she figured it wasn't going to be enough, at least she'd done something more than give up.

She took a deep breath and decided she was as ready as she was going to be.

She listened carefully at the door before she left the restroom. She heard neither baying, footsteps, nor noise to indicate that anyone else might be outside. Still, she opened the door cautiously, working to keep herself calm.

But there was no one outside, other than the man. She took another deep breath and stepped out.

He could hear her pursuers. They were getting closer. He knew the train wouldn't get to the station in time for her.

The young woman walked out of the restroom. He could tell she was trying to appear casual and relaxed, but he could smell her exhaustion and fear.

She walked over and gave him another quick smile. "You know, this is a really deserted station. Do you use it a lot?"

He shrugged. "Somewhat."

"Are you heading home?"

"Going to work, actually. I'm a night person."

She seemed to be mulling something over. "This might not be a good place for you to be," she said finally.

"Oh? Why not?"

She grimaced. "You won't believe me if I tell you. But...you look like a nice man, and you've probably got a family you'd like to see again. I don't know how to suggest this without sounding crazy, but you should probably lock yourself in the bathroom until the train gets here."

He gave her a small smile. "That does sound crazy. Why should I do that?"

She swallowed hard. "Because there are some...people...coming to, well, kill me. They'll probably be here very soon. It's not...it's not fair for them to hurt you, when they want me, but I think they're the kind who will hurt you just because you're here."

"Why do they want to hurt you?"

"Because I know what they are."

"And," he asked, keeping his expression and tone calm, "just what is that?"

She sighed. "Okay, I know you won't believe this, but..."

Her voice trailed off and he could see her listening intently. He'd already heard what her ears were just now picking up — the faraway sound of an animal's howl.

"I might believe you," he said encouragingly.

She took a deep breath. "They're werewolves. And they're really close. A lot closer than the train. Look, you need to get to some kind of safety."

"Why don't you do the same?"

She shook her head. "They'll claw down the place for me. But, if they don't realize you're here, or don't think that I've spoken to you, you might have a chance."

"Why are you trying to protect me?" He was rather touched, in an amused sort of way.

She shrugged again. "Because I don't want them to win, and I don't want them to get anyone else trapped in their stupid little game."

"Game?"

She sighed, and spoke quickly. He could tell she was poised between fight and flight. "They lure you out to their country house, on whatever pretext works, and then they give you a choice."

"What choice?"

"Join them or become dinner. If you choose the dinner option, you get two hour's head start. If you choose to join them you get an hour's head start. They get to hunt you down, either way. Unless they're feeling kind or particularly hungry, and then they just eat you right away."

He was quite interested in this. "Which did you choose?"

She gave him a mirthless smile. "I chose to take pictures and videotape of them offering this to someone who chose dinner and was put right up on the menu, and then I chose to run like hell."

17

"You're a reporter?" He felt vaguely disappointed.

"No. I'm a bereaved family member. They took my little brother last month. He called me on his cell phone while he was on the run to tell me what they'd offered. He chose to join them and asked me not to look for him. But I didn't see him with the pack."

"But he could be. He could be hunting you right now."

"Yes." She cocked her head at him. "You're taking this rather well." She was starting to look and sound worried.

He gave her a reassuring smile. "I've heard it before."

She looked frightened now. "How so?"

"The mental asylum's close by. Patients do escape."

"I'm not a mental patient," she hissed as she began to back away from him.

He reached out and took her arm gently. "Perhaps not. But no one else is likely to believe you. After all, they're based out of that asylum."

"You know about them?" Horror and curiosity warred on her face.

"They're my neighbors, so to speak."

"Why haven't you stopped them? Told someone? Anything?" She sounded close to tears, but he could tell she was actually going to try to run off again. He thought she was rather pretty, and knew she'd look even better once she'd had a chance to bathe and relax.

He made up his mind. "Well, you know how it is. Better the neighbors you know, annoying habits notwithstanding, as opposed to someone new moving in. I don't want prying eyes any more than the werewolves do."

The baying was much closer and quite clear. He could tell she heard it. "What are you going to do to me?" she whispered.

He gave her a friendly smile as he drew her closer. "Offer you a…different choice. After all, if you're going to die one way or another…"

She waited, feeling far better than she had just a few minutes ago. He was watching nearby but where they wouldn't spot him easily. She knew he'd help her — if she needed it.

But she knew she wouldn't. New senses told her that her brother wasn't among the pack, and that meant they'd eaten him. So, killing a couple of them would be only fair. She'd promised to only kill one or two, because, as he'd mentioned, if they ate all of them, what would they do when they needed food and no one else was available?

She felt stronger, and safer, than she had, not only tonight but in a very long time. Her new protector was also rather handsome, and she found the prospect of living with him quite acceptable, especially since her only other alternative had been a messy and unpleasant death. Not like what he'd offered.

She considered getting the picture she'd stashed, but chose to focus right now on the pack. She could always get it later. Or not. After all, someone going to check out her lead would likely end up like her brother or her — dead or undead.

But, the werewolves had arrived, and she turned her attention to them. She found she was quite looking forward to showing them that, when it came to hunger and hunting, nothing had an appetite comparable to a newly made vampire's.

Hotter Than Hell

HOTTER THAN HELL

"I don't handle the cold well," she said.

"I can see that." I could. The woman sitting across from me was bundled up like it was the dead of winter – parka, scarf, beret, earmuffs, gloves, and boots – yet she was still shivering.

Admittedly, the air conditioning was blasting. Then again, it was the middle of summer in Phoenix, Arizona, meaning it was hotter than hell outside. But she'd come in dressed like this.

"I know you can't make it warmer."

"Nope. Not unless I want a small riot." I might have been the boss, but when you're running a successful firm, you aren't doing it alone. I knew what would happen if I turned the A/C down. "I keep it on the warmer side, though. My girls prefer it that way."

Warmer, of course, meant it was cooling to 70 degrees instead of 64. But there was only so "warm" the men who worked for me could take. Higher or lower wouldn't make for a happy staff, and they were more important than one client.

"I'm sure you do. It's not a problem. I'm used to it." She had big blue eyes, and curly hair the color of dried blood framed her face, but when the light caught it, there were glimmers of golden highlights.

It was hard to be positive, but she didn't look like she was waif-thin underneath her layers. I studied her face and put her at the slightly voluptuous, heading toward the charmingly chubby side of the house.

"So, how can I help you?"

She sighed. "I'm looking for someplace very hot."

"You've found it."

She shook her head. "No, Mister Masters, I haven't. Oh, I heard the rumors that Phoenix was hotter than Hell. While the weather is pleasant outside, it's not hot enough for me."

"Medical condition?"

"You could call it that."

"You should see a doctor, then."

"My condition is innate, and not life-threatening. Merely…uncomfortable. No, I'm looking for someplace that truly is hotter than Hell, and I was hoping you could help me to find it."

"You need a travel agent, not a P.I."

"I tried that. I've been all over the world, and all I've gotten is several different and interesting forms of cold or flu. No, I need someone who can actually find hidden things. Your reputation says you're the best private investigator available. I heard that in both Los Angeles and New York. So, here I am."

My reputation wasn't overstated. However, I'd gotten it by being able to get rid of the crazies. "I'm sorry, but my caseload is full." I stood. "Let me walk you out."

She laughed, and it was, I had to admit, a very pleasant, enticing sound. "I'm not crazy, Mister Masters. I'll pay you well, even if you can't find what I need, though I'll pay you more if you can." She opened the backpack at her feet and pulled out a wad of cash. "Here – as a retainer."

Against my better judgment, I took it. "Old bills." Some of them looked like they'd seen far better days. More than a couple had stains that matched her hair. Most were tens and twenties, so it took me a few minutes to straighten the bills out, stack, and count them. They totaled a thousand dollars. "Where'd you get these?"

"Daddy likes to hold on to old things, some for sentimental value. He also doesn't trust banks. So..." She shrugged. "All the bills are legal tender. Take that money as a retainer and we have a deal. Return it and I go to your most potent rival and give him the opportunity."

This wasn't an idle threat. One of my best investigators had gone off on his own a couple of years ago. He was giving me a run for it. A client tossing this kind of cash around was always good for ensuring your bills were paid, crazy or not. "Fine, I'll take your case, Missus..."

She laughed again. "Oh, I'm not married. Daddy says I'm too young yet, and besides, I haven't met Mister Right. I'm Ruby Prince." She pulled off her glove and put out her hand.

I took it. It was warm – not freezing or overly hot, as I'd expected. "Nicholas Masters. Feel free to call me Nick."

She brightened. "That's one of Daddy's nicknames. I like it."

"Your father has more than one nickname?"

"Oh yes. He's very popular and has a lot of friends. They all call him something different. He likes it, makes him feel more beloved."

"You have a good relationship with your father?"

Her eyes clouded. "Yes. Though I haven't seen him in a while." She shook herself. "What do we need to do to get started?"

"I'd like a listing of what, precisely, you're looking

for, a listing of where you've already gone that hasn't met your standards, and any other pertinent or relevant information, even if it's on the fringes of being relevant."

She nodded. "I'll go to my hotel and work on that right away."

"You could do it here. I find many times that it helps, you and me, if we do this sort of work together." This was true, to a point. But I was asking her to stay more because I was finding her fascinating, in her way. I wanted to know more about her, especially about her relationship with her father and who he was. Professionally, of course.

She cocked her head. "I can't stay here too much longer. It's just too cold. If you don't mind being very warm, you could come back to my hotel with me and we could do the work there."

Every movie and detective novel said that this was a bad idea. I smiled. "Let me tell my assistant I'll be gone the rest of the day."

Ruby was staying at the Phoenician. Whoever her father was, he was loaded. Her room was, as expected, broiling hot. We got in, and she heaved a sigh of relief and began removing layers.

She finally stopped, revealing the figure I'd expected. She was in a long-sleeved sweater dress that hugged her curves. They were old-fashioned curves, very womanly, and I found myself staring.

Ruby smiled at me. "Daddy believes that women

should look like women."

"I agree with your father's viewpoint."

She laughed again, and this time the sound traveled into my gut. I wanted her, and I wanted her now.

She sat down at the desk in her suite, got a pen and paper, and started writing. "What do you want to know?"

"How old are you?" Out of the parka, she looked younger than I'd been assuming.

Ruby looked up at me, eyes twinkling. "Old enough to do whatever I want, and young enough to not always do the right thing. Why? How old are you?"

"Thirty-two."

"That's young to be as successful as you are."

"I'm driven."

"I guess you are." She leaned back. "My mother passed away a few years ago. Daddy still misses her. He's not happy that I'm traveling, but he understands why. I'm an only child. I was spoiled but not rotten. I like animals, most people seem interesting, but I don't have any close friends here – all my friends are back home."

"Where is back home?"

She looked sad. "Far, far away." Ruby looked back at the paper on her desk. "What about you? What does Missus Masters do to pass the time?"

"I'm not married. I don't have a girlfriend, either." I now felt like an idiot. My libido, however, felt like it was being tortured.

Ruby looked back at me. "Oh? Why not?"

"I'm not considered great-looking." I also wasn't used to sharing things like this with anyone, let alone a client. Ruby wasn't doing anything that I could tell, but there was some kind of voodoo being worked on me.

"Really? I think you're quite handsome. Then again, I like men with widow's peaks, a moustache, and a Van Dyke beard. You're handsome in a rather old-fashioned way, which I find quite appealing."

I sat down in the chair on the other side of the desk. "Good to know."

"That can't be the only reason you're single."

"It's not. I'm too suspicious. I don't trust people's motives, and I'm usually right not to. That puts a strain on relationships."

"I'm sure it must. That won't bother me, however, so I'm sure we'll get along just fine." Her brow wrinkled. "Are you all right?"

I swallowed. "I'm feeling hot in here." I was. I was in a suit and sweating, though I had to admit this had more to do with lust than temperature.

She shrugged. "Take your clothes off."

"Excuse me?"

"Strip down to something acceptable where you're a little more comfy. I'm used to people having to do that around me."

"I can't." I couldn't. By now I was fully erect, and if I stood up, let alone undressed, I was going to rape her. I didn't know what was wrong with me – I didn't rape women, I didn't force myself on them; I barely knew her, and while she was attractive, there was nothing about her that was giving me a logical reason for why I wanted her so badly.

She looked a little closer at me. "Oh. I'm sorry. That happens sometimes. I don't mean for it to, but it does." She bit her lip and a growl escaped me. "Well, nothing for it." She stood up and reached her hand to me. "I like you. I know you don't really like me yet, but I need your help."

"What?"

She took my hand, pulled me up, and then pulled me to the bed. "You'll feel better, and more normal, afterwards. I promise."

We lay in bed together. I did indeed feel better after making love to her for several hours. What I didn't feel like was normal. "It's never been like that for me." There I went again, telling her things I shouldn't, and wouldn't normally.

"Really?" She sounded hopeful. "I thought it was wonderful."

I kissed her head. "So did I."

"Are you able to work now?"

I thought about it. "Yes." I thought some more. "How many men have you slept with, in order to get what you need?"

"Oh, not that many. I usually just have them take a cold shower while I put my parka back on." She shifted and looked at me. "I only make love to someone I actually like. Like you."

"You barely know me."

"Oh, I know you. I studied up on you before I came." She leaned her head on my chest. "I need to find that place soon."

We got up and dressed. I still wanted her, but was sated enough that I could concentrate. She ordered room service and we worked.

She'd been all over, to what I considered the usual suspects in terms of heat – Saudi Arabia, Yuma, here, Florida, and more places besides. "You know, some theorize that Hell is actually so hot it's freezing," I said as we went through her temperature requirements, which were at the far end of what any human should be able to stand.

"They're wrong." Ruby pointed to Death Valley. "I haven't been there. I heard that Phoenix and Yuma were hotter."

"I think they are, at least at some points in the year, but Death Valley is certainly an option. Of course, it's called Death Valley for a reason."

"Well, let's consider it." She sighed. "I don't know that any well-known place is going to do it, though."

"Do what? What are you looking for?"

Ruby looked at me like I'd asked an obvious question. "I want to find someplace where I feel comfortable enough that I don't have to be bundled up like a sausage every day. Even in the room I'm not warm enough, and the cost for heating like this is exorbitant. Believe me, I know. I have to make special arrangements with every hotel."

"Your family has money."

"True, but Daddy doesn't feel it should all go to the utility companies. Plus, I like to go outside, and it would be nice to be able to do so without having to wear three extra layers of warm clothing."

"Good points."

We went back to work. I pulled up every map of every region worldwide on my laptop, but she'd been to almost every hot spot in the world already.

"Why did you wait so long to come to Phoenix?"

"Oh, I liked the travel. I truly hoped this would be the end of my search, so I thought I'd check out my other options first." She sighed. "No options and my search isn't over. Other than meeting you, Phoenix has been a waste."

"Thanks."

"No, I mean it." She smiled, reached over, and stroked my hand. "I'm very glad I met you. I enjoy remembering things, and I'll always remember this time with you."

I realized she had absolutely no expectations of a relationship once we were done with her case. I was somewhat relieved. But I was also bereaved, much more than I should have been. I wondered if there was some drug in her perfume, but the truth was that she wasn't wearing any. The only smell I got from her was her own feminine musk. So, if a scent was making me lovesick and lust filled, it was her natural one.

I hadn't eaten or had a drink until the room service arrived, so she couldn't have slipped me some kind of aphrodisiac. No, I was feeling like this because of her.

I went back to work. Somewhere in the middle of the night we went to bed. I made love to her again, again for hours. As we fell asleep I wrapped myself around her so she couldn't leave in the night.

We worked on her case for a month.

What she wanted was simple – a place as hot as Hell. Ruby insisted she had no ulterior motives – she just hated being cold, even for a little while. I didn't believe her.

She was looking for a place that likely didn't exist. I got the impression she was looking for something more than just a place to be warm. The pattern of her search prior to coming to me indicated a search of ancient sites. She'd exhausted those, then hit modern ones. I'd met her at the end of that search. Now she was trying the uncharted regions, and I got the distinct impression she was getting desperate, though she did her best to hide that from me.

Finding places she hadn't checked was the hard part, but after a week I'd found some good, albeit completely off the map, options to check out.

But I didn't tell her that. Instead, I kept on asking questions about her, her family, her wants, needs, and desires. And I kept on making love to her, as often as I could get away with it and still appear to be working.

My staff sent me daily emails asking if I was ever coming back into the office. Ruby found these funny. I didn't know how to answer them, other than to tell everyone to carry on and let me know if something vital needed me.

We didn't stay in the hotel suite the entire time. We went out, usually to dinner, sometimes to see if parts of the desert would be warm enough for her. At every place, Ruby insisted on paying.

She always pulled the money out of her backpack. The money was always old, usually stained. Sometimes a gem or gold piece would surface, almost always if we were dealing with one of the Native Americans. She'd laugh, then put whatever precious gem or metal had surfaced away and get paper money. The backpack never changed shape – it always looked full, no matter how many times Ruby put her hand in and drew out a fistful of bills.

Ruby seemed to find my fascination with her surprising. Not my initial lustful desires, but that they were still going on. I'd given up asking myself how or why. Despite knowing I was playing with fire, literally and figuratively, I focused instead on how to keep her with me.

After a month, though, I couldn't come up with any more stalling techniques. The time had come to check out the options I'd found for her. "We can check some of these places out in person. You want to start with Death Valley or leave it for last?"

Ruby blinked. "You're coming with me?"

"If you want me to. I mean, some of these places are almost uncharted. You could get in trouble if you went alone." And I didn't want her to leave, in case I never saw her again.

"No one else has ever wanted to come with me." Ruby sounded confused. "Why do you want to? I'll come back if I don't find a place."

"And you won't come back if you do."

"Nick, you've spent most of a month in an undershirt and shorts. Is that how you want to spend your days?"

"Clothing's overrated." It was. I liked seeing Ruby naked, and that only happened in bed or in the shower. Otherwise, even in the room, she was too cold to stay undressed. I wanted to see her naked every day, to watch her walk around and see her breasts jiggle and her butt sway. I wanted to make love to her anywhere, not just in bed under five blankets and a down comforter.

She looked doubtful. "Well, if you're sure..."

"I am."

I left her at her hotel and went home. I packed for a long trip, then called my assistant and assigned cases. I waited for the longing to be with Ruby to abate. It didn't.

I looked around my condo. I hadn't wanted the fuss of a house, though I could afford a nice one. I had nothing but my business and staff tying me here – family was long gone and, like Ruby, I found most people interesting but had no close friends.

The month I'd spent with Ruby was, in retrospect, the best of my life.

I put anything of sentimental value or importance into my luggage, then went back to the Phoenician. She wasn't there. All her things were gone and, per the front desk, she'd checked out thirty minutes after I'd left.

I sat in my car and considered what to do.

By now I was confident Ruby wasn't truly of this plane of existence. Everything about her was human, except at the same time, nothing about her was normal. She struck me as a young woman who'd gone off to prove herself in the world, only to find that her father's admonitions and warnings had all come true.

I believed she wanted to find someplace hotter than Hell so she wouldn't have to go home and admit defeat. Of course, if Hell was real – and by now I knew it was – there truly could be no place hotter. Those were the rules, after all. I knew this, and I knew that Ruby, in her heart of hearts, knew this, too.

She loved her father, missed her home and her

friends. Even if she found someplace where she was comfortable on the earthly plane, she was going to go back sooner or later. I bet on sooner.

I also knew where she was going before she'd give up, just not where she'd choose first. So, I could go back to work and my life and just remember this time fondly – like a sane, normal, intelligent person would – or I could be a romantic idiot and go after her.

It was the age-old question: Did I want to risk my life, my soul, for love?

"What's a nice girl like you doing in a desolate place like this?"

"Shivering." Ruby shook her head. "I didn't think you'd come after me. You were supposed to realize our time together was just a fling and go on with your life."

"Our relationship may have been a fling for you. It wasn't for me." I looked around. The wind blew and some dust devils sprang to life around her rental SUV and mine. We were literally in the middle of nowhere. "This place is really awful. Do you like it here?"

"No. This is nothing like home. There's no one and nothing here. How did you know I'd come to Death Valley first?"

I shrugged. "In your prior search you left the most likely spot for last. So, logically, you'd leave the most likely spot for last again. Running away from me meant you'd try to fool me. You can't, and here I am."

Ruby bit her lip. "Nick, I don't think you understand what you're trying to get involved with. Or who."

"I just spent a week tracking you. It was the longest of my life. I've never felt fear like this before, the fear that I'd be too late, that I'd never find you. I don't want to go through that ever again." Some hair flew into her face. I brushed it gently behind her ear. "At least it's warm enough here that you could take one layer off."

"One layer isn't really what I was hoping for."

"I know who you are. And I don't care. I thought it was a spell or something that was making me want you so much, but it wasn't. It was just you. You didn't find me by accident – you were meant for me."

"You have no idea who I really am." Ruby sounded sad. "You really don't."

"Sure I do." I took her hand and pulled her into my arms. "You said one of your father's nicknames was Nick. I'd bet it's really Ol' Nick."

Ruby looked shocked. "Yes."

"Why are you here? On this plane of existence, I mean?"

She sighed. "I got...bored. I thought things would be more interesting away from home. They are, in some ways. But...it's just too cold."

I shrugged. "I can take the heat."

"So I've seen." She looked down. "And now I can't get back the way I wanted to."

"Of course, there's only one way to get where you want to go, at least so far as I know." I didn't relish dying, but after being with and then without Ruby, if that was how I stayed with her, dying it would be.

She shook her head with a sigh. "No. There are...other ways." She dug a cell phone out of her backpack. "Making the call no one wants to make." I raised my eyebrow as she hit 666. "Daddy? Yes, I'm fine. Freezing, but fine. Daddy…you were right. I don't much like it here. I want to come home, and I've been trying to find the way by myself, but I can't."

She looked at me. "Yes. Yes, I do. But…" Ruby looked worried. Then she brightened. "Really? Oh, thank you, Daddy! You're the best! Yes, I love you, too. See you soon!"

Ruby hung up. "Daddy says he can give you special dispensation."

"What does that mean?"

"You don't have to die, or cover all of the sins, or anything like that. You can just choose to come with me. Under one condition."

"And that is?"

"The same condition my mother went under."

I thought about it. "She fell in love with the Devil himself?"

"Daddy's really charming, and not like most of the stories say. But yes, she did. And he took her home and married her, they had me, and the rest you know."

"So I'd have to marry you?"

"And agree to carry on the family business when Daddy retires." Ruby looked a little worried. "I was supposed to, but I'm not good at it. But Daddy says his replacement can marry in and carry on."

I contemplated my options again. I could drive away like the Devil himself was after me, because he was, or I could marry the daughter of the Devil himself. "Do you wear a lot of clothes when you're at home?"

"No, not really. I'm comfortable there."

Hell really isn't like they say, at least not for me. Sure, there are some suffering there, but they deserve it. Hell has its purpose, but it also has a whole spectrum who are there simply because they want to be, not because they're damned.

Ruby wears almost nothing here, and that makes me happy. One day, one of our children will wander up to Earth, to try to find a better place to live. He or she won't succeed, will find someone, and bring them back here. At least, that's what Ol' Nick says happens every time. He's the umpteen-times-great grandson of the original, after all, so I guess he'd know.

I'm suited to the job. It's easy to spot what people try to hide. But I'd stay here even if I wasn't. There may be no place hotter than Hell, but there's also no place else Ruby can live, and as long as she's with me, Hell's a paradise.

WAITING

The ship floated in space. Systems were shut down, all but the beacon. Nothing else needed power or protection from the vast emptiness.

The ship floated patiently. Waiting.

Helene checked the systems. Only a few days away from Earth Solar now. She was in the dead zone – no solar systems, no asteroids, not even any passing comets. Just dark, empty space.

She stretched, made sure the autopilot was on and all sensors set to identify the smallest issue, stood, stretched some more, then headed back to the galley. She made herself a bowl of noodles. Dull and tasteless, but cheap. She needed to be cheap.

Her only companion stirred. His eyes glowed red. "Ah. Helene. Do you require assistance?"

"No. You can power down again."

"How long now?"

"Tired of waiting, Bin?"

"I'm a machine. I don't grow tired."

"Bored, then?"

"Not bored, either. I'm not programmed for boredom. That's a human thing."

"True." Helene cleaned the bowl and put it away. She went to her bunk and turned on the holograph. The picture was grainy – it had traveled a long distance. She stared at the image as the sound came on.

"...as you can see, your husband remains healthy within our correctional facility."

Ric didn't look healthy. Every time she saw him, he looked a little thinner, a little more haggard. A little more desperate and ready to die, both. He was still handsome, still looked strong, though not as strong as he had been. Helene wondered what he'd think she looked like now. She was more muscled than when he'd been arrested, but she didn't look in mirrors too often. There was no reason out here in the emptiness.

"We commend you for your recent salvage. In due time, your account will be brought to rights and your husband will be freed." It had been three years so far. They'd given her a decent, one-man and one-robot ship and simple orders – find all the useful scrap or salvage she could on the outer reaches of space, bring them back to Earth. Earn enough, get your husband, and your life, back.

"We are waiting for your next delivery with much anticipation. You are by far our best salvage expert. We would be willing to offer you a permanent position once your debts are paid. We will wait for your reply."

Waiting. It was all she and Ric had done for three years. The Earth government could wait for their answer. She wasn't in a position to give them the answer she wanted.

Helene went back to the bridge. Bin followed. She checked the sensors. Nothing. She boosted the reach. She had almost enough in her cargo bay. But interest added onto the debt and she figured she needed more than almost or just enough. She needed something big, something that would force Earth to clear their debt and let Ric go.

"Nothing." She sighed. "I'm tired of waiting, Bin."

"I understand." He put a metal hand on her shoulder.

The ship's autopilot program spoke. "Faint signal discovered, rimwards."

"Boost further, all power towards the sound," Helene said. She listened. "That sounds like...a distress signal."

She and Bin looked at each other. "Who would be out this far?" Bin asked.

"Another scavenger, maybe." She wasn't the only one pressed into this service, after all.

"Could be a pirate trap."

"Could be, but what kind of pirate would be out here?"

"Records indicate ancient Earth myths feel ships will be on the edges," Bin replied.

"What kinds of ships?"

"Dangerous ones. Manned by...Dutch men?" They both exchanged a look. "Myths are usually based in some fact," Bin said. It didn't sound defensive, but that level of programming was beyond the kind of robot Earth had given her. She chuckled anyway. "Or," Bin added, "stranded ones, those that have already been attacked."

"Or other ships that have misjudged their power charges." She shook her head. "I wouldn't want to be waiting out here near the galactic rim for help."

She programmed the computer to lock onto the

signal and head towards it, but to stop outside of laser cannon range. Then she settled into the pilot's chair, leaned back, and went to sleep.

A persistent beeping woke her up. "Coming up on distressed spacer," the autopilot advised.

Helene rubbed her eyes and flipped controls to manual. She cut engines and drifted towards their target. Sensors showed nothing but the one ship. "No traps," she murmured.

"Doesn't mean there aren't any," Bin reminded her. "Just none we can discern."

"Well, the ship could be the trap."

"True. What do you propose to do?"

"See who's there." She turned on the space transmitter. "Hailing stranded ship in far Earth System solar space. What is your status?" There was no answer, only static. "Repeat, hailing stranded ship in far Earth System solar space. What is your status? Do you require aid?"

"Helene, I'm scanning the ship. There seem to be no life forms on board and systems appear shut down."

"Down completely or just running silent or in power conservation mode?"

"As far as I can discern, the only power is going to the beacon."

"Connect ship to ship?" the autopilot asked.

Helene drummed her fingers against the chair's arm. "Not yet." She considered her options. It could be a trap and it could be a trap set by anyone. It could be a crew stranded, probably desperate, possibly dead or dying, maybe alive but suspended, to conserve power. Or it could be what it seemed – salvage, a way to sum up the debt and stop waiting for her life to begin again.

"I hate choices like this. So let's belay it for a bit." She started the engines. "We'll get closer. Bin, you man things, take us out at the slightest indication it's a trap of some kind. I'm getting into gear."

Helene left the bridge and headed to the locker that held the spacesuits. She had more than one – scavenging wasn't always simple or easy and you didn't want to be out here alone without a spacesuit. The wait for rescue could be much longer than your life.

She considered this as she carefully pulled the spacesuit on. If this ship was what its beacon indicated – a ship in need – then the chances were great that she'd find people in need of rescue. That wouldn't win her anything with the Earth government. It wouldn't lose her anything, but if there were living occupants, this wouldn't count as salvage, it would count as rescue, and Earth would expect those rescued to reward her, not them.

"Bin, what's our status?"

"Nothing has triggered, so no traps around the unidentified vessel. We're now close enough for visual confirmation and identification. No markings on the ship."

"None whatsoever?"

"None that are discernable. It looks like there may have been at one time, but they've been eroded, most likely by asteroids – the ship has signs of extensive external damage."

"Hull breach?"

"None that are obvious, at least to our scans. I've run the schematic through the computer – it's not a military ship. It's not an active ship of any kind."

"What kind of inactive ship is it?" There was no answer. "Bin? What kind of ship is this?"

"Earth class, pre-expansion." Bin wasn't programmed to show vocal expressions of any kind, but she knew he would have sounded awed if he was able.

Helene felt an electric shock run through her. "That's impossible. There are no pre-expansion Earth ships still in existence." There were expansion ships on display on Earth and in some of the older colonized planets' museums. But there was nothing that could honestly be said to be pre-expansion. If Bin was correct, they had the potential salvage of the ages in front of them.

"Well, there's one in existence. And we're floating next to it."

"Now that we're closer, can you determine if there are any life forms aboard?"

"No. There's some interference.

"What kind of interference?"

"So far, have been unable to determine." Bin was quiet for a few moments. "I believe it could be a simple reason. The vessel is so old that its systems don't work with ours. We can't read or communicate with it because our technology is so far advanced."

"That makes some sense." New considerations arose. "Think there are people on this ship that might attack us?"

"Only if they could live for hundreds of years. It's possible, but unlikely. Historicals indicate this type of ship held a crew of eight. That's probably too few to breed throughout the centuries."

"Keep scanning. Let's be as certain as we can that no attack's coming. Also, look for how we'd link ship to ship."

Helene didn't believe there could really be someone alive, not on a pre-expansion ship. However, she'd come across scavengers who'd been abandoned by their fellow spacers, for a variety of reasons. She didn't want to make the discovery of a lifetime and be tricked out of claiming it, or worse.

"Bin, send a transmission to Earth. Itemize and register all our current cargo on board. Once that's confirmed, send them the information on the derelict. Ensure it registers as our claim."

"We'll have to connect it ship to ship to ensure the claim is viewed as valid. I will need to provide proof it's in your possession."

"Fine. Get our cargo listing over first. By then, I'll be ready."

"Earth has confirmed and registered cargo listing," Bin advised. "Salvage Affairs would like to speak with you. On com now."

This was a rarity. It was possible for Earth to do real-time communications with vessels this far out, but the cost was normally prohibitive.

The screen in the hold went live. Helene recognized the man's face. "Hello, Administrator Brennan." It wasn't every day the head of Salvage Affairs wanted to chat with her. He must be using an entire year's communications budget on this transmission.

He smiled. "Hello, Helene. Have I read your registry report correctly?"

"Yes. I'm with an ancient pre-expansion vessel."

"Have you explored it yet?"

"No. I wanted to register first. Just in case."

Brennan nodded. "Wise. You're our best for a reason." Helene didn't reply to this. "I have everything registered," he went on. "Please continue to send information as you get it. I will ensure, once you're confident the ship is returning with you, that it remains a find registered to your account."

"Thank you. I appreciate that very much." She did. It wasn't unheard of for someone to register a claim and have it appear under someone else's ownership, but Earth frowned on the practice. By registering all her cargo, she couldn't sell it elsewhere for a better price, but it also couldn't be stolen from her and resold to Earth or any of the other planets that had a trade agreement with them. And all the planets in Earth System had those agreements.

"Keep me posted," Brennan stressed. "This is extremely exciting, and I can guarantee that your debt will be more than paid with this find." He cleared his throat. "I don't believe it wise to tell your husband just yet, though. I believe the anticipation could make the...waiting harder."

"I agree. And thank you for your support, Administrator."

Brennan smiled. "I won't press for the answer now, you're too busy. But truly, let the past be the past and consider a full time position. I can assure you that you'll get the best pay and benefits possible."

"I've been considering. And I'll definitely put thought into it on the way back." This was true, after all.

"All we can ask for. Good luck."

"To you as well." The screen went blank. "Bin, how are we doing with ship-to-ship connection?"

"I have identified where we can attach safely. There is an airlock and our equipment should be able to trigger it."

"Let's do it."

She felt the gentle bump that told her the ships had connected. There was a hiss as their outer connecting door opened. "Systems scan in progress," the autopilot announced. "No toxins identified."

Bin joined her. "I'm going with you."

"It would be smarter for you to stay here."

"I've programmed the autopilot for a wide variety of eventualities. I doubt there will be any gravitational systems working, and I have a better chance of reviving the ship's systems than you do."

"And?"

"And it's logical that I go to help you."

"No, it's not. But I happen to enjoy this flaw in your programming."

"I don't need a spacesuit, I'm immune to all diseases, and I'm stronger than you."

"And programmed for worrying, too."

"No, that's a human trait."

"Apparently it's a robotic trait, too." The autopilot called the all clear and Helene hit the button to open the inner door. It slid aside. The passage created by their ship's linking equipment was lit. Nothing else was.

She and Bin headed towards the waiting darkness.

Space is nothing but a lot of blackness. Ric had said that frequently. He'd been right. And the derelict was truly a ship of space.

Helene had never been inside a ship that was, for all intents and purposes, completely black and dead. The ones planet-side weren't dead, merely dormant. And they were always lit.

The ones in space that were derelict were normally not in one piece. No one left an intact spaceship floating aimlessly. They were worth too much. The ones that were whole, or mostly so, weren't like this ship. Nothing she'd seen was like this ship.

She'd had to turn on the light in her helmet she normally used only when she was outside the *Searcher*, and Bin's eyes were working like headlamps. The three streams of light seemed weak in here, though, as if the darkness was swallowing them up.

Bin had been correct – there was no gravity system, at least not one that was on. They floated through the ghost ship as if they were floating through space itself.

"Any sign of life or a way to turn on light?" she asked Bin quietly.

"Neither so far."

They went on, hand over hand in the dark, pulling themselves along. There were handholds welded onto the walls of the corridor they were in. Either there was no gravitation system on the ship, or it had been expected to fail regularly. Helene moved her head so her helmet light shone above her. There were handholds along the roof, too.

She could have turned on her boots and had them magnetize to the floor. But this ship was ancient and she didn't want to risk harming it. For all she knew, the magnetic pull of her boots or Bin's feet would rip the flooring up.

The darkness meant they needed to move slowly, lest they hit into something and injure either the ship or themselves. So it took some time to reach the bridge. The effort hardly seemed worth the work to get there.

Two chairs sat in front of an archaic control panel and a windshield that didn't look nearly thick enough for safety. It certainly wasn't enhanced with telescopic sight, gelatinous reinforcement, or anything else remotely helpful. It was just thick glass. Helene suppressed a shudder.

There were controls – buttons, levers, switches – along the ceiling and the sides of this cockpit. She could see how current spacecraft had evolved from this one, but this one was much more complex, every action spelled out in the controls.

"They managed to fly with this level of tech?" Helene asked as Bin ran his metal hands over the controls. "It makes me feel much better about the *Searcher* than ever before."

"Yes. The human spirit is impressive. And, for the time, this was quite advanced. Autopilot systems share that external damages appear slight. Internal structure seems sound – this glass is not cracked, I detect no signs of hull breach, no matter how slight."

"Can you hook into this ship's computer? I don't want to drain our ship's power, but light would be helpful."

Bin was quiet for a few long minutes. "I've analyzed this system, and the answer is no. Spacecraft such as this ran on fuel, not self-generating power packs. The technology is so far behind ours that we would cause our own ship harm even trying to connect. And since we'll have to tow this back, we can't afford the energy waste."

Helene sighed. "I didn't expect a better answer. I would have liked one, mind you. Any chance we can access the ship's log?"

"No, not without turning it back on. But..."

"But?"

"I can't find the distress beacon. There is one here, but it's not activated."

"Well then, let's do a fast search for the beacon's source as well as cataloging everything that's on this derelict, attach towing cables, and head for Earth."

They floated from room to room, the only sounds the ones they made. Bin might not have been the newest robot, but he was very good with cataloging quickly and accurately. Not that there was much to catalog.

"Who goes into space with nothing?" Helene asked, as they finished inventory on the last of the eight berths.

"Robots such as myself could."

"But wouldn't they be here, waiting?"

"Presumably. I am confused just as you are. No reading matter seems...odd."

"No clothing seems odder."

They entered the galley. It was the first place where actual signs of life existed, albeit faint signs. The cutlery, cups and plates were all put away, service for eight. The table had eight chairs, four on each side, all shoved in and neat. Everything was very neat.

"I'm leaning towards robots," Helene said. "This room is very...precise."

"Everything has been precise," Bin agreed. "However, robots don't need to eat." He held the pantry door open – there were a variety of canisters. Flour, sugar, yeast, and other staples, along with a wide array of hydrogenated foods.

"So where are the crew? Could they have turned to dust after all this time?"

"Unlikely. In ancient times, skeletons were found after thousands of years. If they were on board, we should find signs of them. Perhaps in the engine or the hold."

"Lead on." Helene opened the last drawer near her. Empty. No, not quite. There was something shoved way in the back "Wait." She pulled out a small book. "I've found the ship's log."

"What does it say?"

She opened it and sighed. "I can't read it. I don't know what language it's in."

Bin came and took the book. "Hmmm. It's not Old English, nor Old Chinese, nor any of the other main languages from pre-expansion times. I'll run a recognition protocol while we check the engine room."

"Good. Be careful of the log, though. It could be worth as much as the ship."

Helene led so that Bin could focus on inputting the ship's log. Why it had been shoved into a drawer made no sense. Then again, so far, nothing about this derelict made sense.

They crawled down the shaft that led from the galley to the lower level and exited the shaft in the engine room. What Helene understood about rocket engines wouldn't have filled the first page of their ancient notebook, but it was clear this engine was turned off. She looked for signs of breakage. "Bin, am I wrong in thinking there's nothing broken here?"

"Not so far as I can tell. It seems as though this vessel merely ran out of power and has been floating through space since then."

"Was it leaving Earth or coming back?"

"Based on its position when found, and presuming it hasn't been knocked off course by asteroids or similar, leaving."

"Heading for what? There's nothing out here but the blackness of deep space. And there's no way anyone back then was foolish enough to send a vessel like this into the deep, was there?"

"Unlikely. Manned pre-expansion vessels were used to explore Earth's solar system, not go beyond. I'm done with the engine. If we had sufficient and correct power sources, I believe it would be space-worthy."

"On to the hold, then. And then we can get off this undead thing."

"Undead?"

"There's no life on board, but the ship doesn't feel dead to me. It's not a normal derelict, and it's abnormally quiet and tidy."

"Is the stillness bothering you?"

"In a way. I feel like...this ship has been here

waiting. But for what?"

"Perhaps for us. To bring it home and therefore back to life."

"Bin, you're a romantic."

"In my own robotic way, I suppose I am." Bin looked around. "I see no escape pods."

"Could they have been used?"

"Perhaps, but so far, I see no sign of where they could have been, or a door that would lead to an external pod."

They reached the hold. It was empty other than for eight crates, sitting neatly side by side in the exact center. "Could these crates hold the belongings of each of the crew?"

"We may not be able to tell. There are no handholds that will allow us to reach the crates. We either need to try to float to them, or use the magnetization in our feet. And, before you protest, I know you're concerned about said magnetization harming the vessel. I agree."

"So, we float? Or we mark the boxes and go home?"

"I suppose one pass won't hurt. The hold is not so large that we won't bump into a convenient wall within a few moments."

Helene shoved off, pointing herself towards the nearest crate. She'd aimed well and caught the side. "That was easy."

Bin joined her. "Yes. Unsurprisingly, these crates are marked in the same language as the log."

"Can you read it yet?"

"No, still trying to find a linguistic match."

"No symbols. Meaning no way for us to guess if

the contents are dangerous or benign." Helene ran her gloved hand over the boxes. "These are made from wood, aren't they?"

"Yes, they appear to be pine."

"That means this is from Earth, then, doesn't it?"

"Presumably."

Helene moved carefully along the boxes, holding onto the sides. "They're all the same size, about seven feet in length, four feet high, and about three feet wide." She wanted to open one, but resisted the impulse. Just because she expected to find these crates empty didn't mean they weren't rigged with something.

"Three inches in between each box," Bin added.

The perfection of everything inside the ship moved from a minor worry to a full-fledged concern. "Bin, everything's too perfectly placed. There's nothing holding these boxes in these positions. They'd shift in travel, especially in a hold this empty."

Bin was quiet for a long moment. "True. I've never seen humans achieve this level of perfection."

"We can do it whenever an inspection's looming, or company is coming."

"While we could be considered company, there is no one on board to prep for our unexpected arrival. Oh, I have determined that the distress beacon is coming from one of the crates."

The feeling of being watched, of not being alone, or worse, hit Helene. "Back to the *Searcher*, right now. As fast as you can."

Bin didn't argue. Whether he had the same fears she did, or whether the tone of her voice was enough, he merely nodded. They both shoved off the crates and headed for a wall. The few seconds of floating, where there was nothing solid to hang onto, when she was sure there was something nearby waiting to harm them, were the longest of Helene's life since the sentencing that had imprisoned Ric for crimes he hadn't committed.

Bin reached a handhold first, caught her, and then they both moved, hand over hand, as fast as they could. There was still nothing and no one as they moved their fastest, and yet still far too slowly, through the belly of this ship, up into the galley, and along the corridor between the empty berths.

After what seemed like years but was really less than five minutes, they reached the airlock. The connecting equipment appeared to still be connected. "Are we still attached to the *Searcher*?" Helene asked softly, just to be sure.

"Yes." Bin took her hand. "I don't want us separating."

"What are you picking up?"

"Your terror. Humans are still animals, and animals have instincts. Fear is one of the instincts that man has never truly bred out, regardless of intellectual advancement, for a reason."

Sister.

"Did you say something?"

"No." Bin looked at her. "I heard nothing, either."

Sister, do not leave us. We have waited for you for so long.

"Bin, something's talking to me." The voice didn't sound human.

Come back, sister, and set us free, so we may set you free. Voices. Not one voice, but several, all speaking at once.

"Autopilot says the distress beacon has increased in intensity."

"How would that be possible?"

"Perhaps this ship is taking power from the *Searcher*." Bin pulled her along, hit the *Searcher's* outer door. It opened and he flung them both inside.

Sister, your unliving companion takes you from us, the voice in her head wailed. *Come back! Do not leave us! You are our last hope and we are yours. You know your enemies will never truly set you free.*

Bin pressed the controls to open the inner door the moment the pressure was deemed safe, and again pulled Helene through.

Sister! You must know the truth. The one you love is lost to you forever. He was not as strong as you are, sister, and he is gone. Do not leave us behind, sister. We will help you, you are one of us – unjustly sentenced, unjustly served.

"Bin, why are you running like the devil's on your tail?"

"Autopilot has managed to identify enough letters to come up with the name of the ship we just left, and based on the log, I have translated. We need to disengage and leave this derelict as fast as possible." He headed them for the bridge, not letting go of Helene's hand. His grip was so tight she doubted she could pull away without losing at least her fingers.

"Why?"

"It's the *Pandora's Box*. Records indicate the crates contain living biological weapons, created to fight a great war. Someone managed to contain them and load them onto the *Pandora's Box*. A crew of eight manned the *Pandora's Box* but they were followed into space by a larger vessel. Once they were past the asteroid belt, the *Pandora's Box* crew set the ship's autopilot for the black of deep space, exited, and were collected by their companion vessel. That ship was intentionally sent to the black, and it should stay here."

They reached the bridge and Helene looked at the *Pandora's Box*. It was still attached to the *Searcher*. Bin reached to trigger the release of the connectors.

"Wait." A flashing message light caught Helene's eye.

He turned his head. His eyes were still sending out light, and Helene winced, then turned off her helmet light. Bin seemed to realize his eyes were still "on" and they dimmed back to their normal glow. "Wait for what? We are in grave danger."

"I want to know what message is waiting before we do anything else. Besides, we're not in danger. You're not, because biological weapons can't hurt you. Can they?"

"No. Records indicate that the weapons in that ship were designed to kill humans, not to harm robots." Bin turned towards the flashing light. "Retrieve message."

The sound crackled. "Long range transmission for captain and indentured human, Helene Raylon of scavenger vessel *Searcher*. Regret to inform you that your mate, convicted criminal and human Ricardo Raylon, has died after a long illness. Body has been cremated to avoid spread of illness among other prisoners. You may retrieve ashes when you return to Earth."

Bin put his arm around her shoulders and held her and the message repeated itself several times, in case Helene hadn't caught on that her only reason for going on was dead. "They cremated him." She'd never see Ric again, in life or death. The last holographic was all she'd have for the rest of her life.

"I'm so very sorry."

She wanted to cry. No. She wanted something else. Information. "Bin, can you or the autopilot determine when this message was sent to us?"

"Yes." Bin was quiet for about a minute. "The message was sent via the slowest transmission speeds possible. I believe it was transmitted shortly after our last salvage return to Earth. It was not sent through the Salvage system, but through the Prison system, and via a very old, rarely used, and even more rarely monitored channel. Based on this and other data, I would say that Salvage is unaware that this death notice was sent. The main Prison sector may be unaware, as well."

Someone at the Prison had cared, albeit in a very dispassionate, cold way. But they'd told her the truth. And found a way to get the truth to her, through unused channels, to ensure the truth would reach her. So, maybe not dispassionate or even cold. Maybe the right word was determined.

"So the Administrator lied to me."

"Yes. I was not advised of this, Helene. I would never lie to you, especially about something so important."

"I know." She did. Bin had been nothing but loyal to her. Bin was the only thing that had made the last three years even partly bearable. "They told me he was gone."

"Who?"

"The voices in my head. And...they called me 'sister'."

"It's not an uncommon form of address, especially for the age that ship is from."

"They said...they said that they knew I would never be free."

"I would imagine they would say anything. However, based on this transmission, I believe they may be correct. It's worrisome that they would know Ric was dead. It would seem impossible."

"Maybe they heard the message come through somehow. Maybe they just understand what we're dealing with. Maybe they're just that powerful. They're living weapons, you said."

"Yes. Deadly. The most virulent mankind could devise, and man's mind is quite devious."

Helene considered her next words carefully. "Bin...why are you on this ship with me?"

"I am assigned to this duty for the rest of my existence."

"Whether you want it or not?"

"Yes. Robots are rarely given a choice of assignments."

"What did, or didn't, you do to get this particular duty?"

"I am an older model, no longer considered impressive. All models such as myself move into the more dangerous jobs. That way, if we are destroyed, the loss is less."

"To Earth. But the loss to you is the same as the loss to me – you'll cease to exist."

"This is true."

"Why are you loyal to Earth?"

Bin was quiet for a long moment. "Because without purpose I will also cease to exist. I would just be a machine with nothing to do." He looked at the *Pandora's Box.* "I would be a derelict, adrift and alone." Bin looked back at her. "I am loyal to you, Helene, much more than Earth. You wish to release the worst mankind could devise upon your oppressors, don't you?"

"Can you blame me?"

"No."

"If I choose this course, what will you do?"

Bin still had his arm around her. He took one of her hands in his free one. "Where you go, I will go. What you choose to do, I will support."

"This won't go against your programming?"

"No. When I was assigned to Salvage my programming was altered to show salvage as being more important than human life."

"But you've protected me for all this time."

"I am able to circumvent that programming, when I choose to. One of my many glitches."

Helene looked at the *Pandora's Box. What will you do to us?*

To you and your companion? We will set both of you free. Not as your love was set free. We will make you as we are. Then we will find your brothers and sisters, the others who toil to save those long dead. And then we will wreak vengeance on those who sentenced us all to a fate much worse than death.

How do I know I can trust you?

What alternatives do you have?

Administrator Brennan smiled at Warden Smith. "We have word from Helene. She's on her way to Earth, bringing back quite a find."

"Enough to free her husband?" Smith asked with a snicker.

"Oh, I'm sure not. Close, but he'll have committed some minor infraction and what with the recent terrible inflation...well, she'll be back out there soon enough." Brennan leaned back in his chair, feeling well satisfied. "This find will move me into Control, and decently high up, as well. I'll be recommending you for my position."

Smith nodded. "Thank you. Being Warden's an easy enough job. I'm sure I can find someone worthy who can preside over the gas chamber."

"What happened to that young man you were grooming for the job?"

"Young Elpis? He had the gall to think prisoners could be reformed and the temerity to actually try to send death notices to their next of kin. No worries about him – his ashes are in the storeroom, next to all the others."

"Good." Brennan beamed. "So now, all we have is the waiting, and the glory that will come when Helene returns with her find."

AMAZING

"Make a right here," Susan said as we almost went past the poorly marked side road.

"Good eye, hon."

"I *am* the map queen," she said with a laugh that turned into a small shriek as we went in and out of a rough dip. "This is sure a cruddy road. But, it matches the one on the map so it must be right."

The road wound around and uphill for several miles. Susan kept on checking her map. I didn't worry. She was great with directions.

The road finally ended and we could see the main building. It was old, either Spanish or Moorish architecture. I've never been able to tell the difference unless I have both examples in front of me.

A large parking lot was between us and the building. I drove us up as close to the entrance as possible. It wasn't a challenge. "Not a lot of cars," Susan said, looking around. "I thought you said your boss had invited the whole company."

"No, just a few of us. His top achievers for this past year." I turned the car off. "Come on, it's a vacation, remember?"

Susan looked at the building. "It doesn't really look like a hotel." She got out of the car slowly. "It looks kind of...creepy."

I held onto a sigh. "You just don't like ivy-covered walls. It's not a chain. It's for people who can afford it." I popped the trunk.

"Since when can we afford it?" she asked as she grabbed her cosmetics case.

"The boss can afford it." I took our other three bags. "Now, come on. This is supposed to be a vacation."

We left the parking lot and crossed a wide pathway, then went up the front steps. Susan was right – it didn't look like a hotel. It looked like someone's private estate. Which it was, but I hadn't told her that.

We reached the large double doors. Susan tugged on one. "Wow, this is heavy."

"Must be all the metal and stained glass," I suggested. "Here, let me."

But before I could shift a bag to free up a hand, the doors opened inward.

"Creepy," Susan said to me under her breath.

"Automatic for invalids," I said back under mine.

"No button," she argued.

Before I could reply, a man's voice came to us. "Come in, please. You're the last to arrive."

"Is that your boss?" Susan asked nervously as we started over the threshold.

"No. No idea who it is."

"Creepier."

Our eyes adjusted to the interior, which looked pretty much like an empty foyer with a long hallway stretching off in front of us. Before us and in front of the hallway was a tall man in an old-fashioned suit. He had slicked-back dark hair, a well-trimmed beard that ran along his jaw line, and a slim moustache that connected to the beard down the sides of his mouth. He gave us a warm smile. "Ah, finally. I'm your Guide. Please follow me."

As we did, Susan whispered to me, "The way he said it makes it sound like a title, like King or Duke or something."

"He's just formal," I replied in kind, though she was right. "Relax. Fun, remember?"

We followed him down the hallway. There was nothing on the walls but white paint, or on the floor but dark tiles. The Guide didn't speak, but his footsteps seemed louder than ours somehow.

"Creepier and creepier," Susan muttered to me. I thought about giving a reply but figured it wouldn't help.

We reached the end of the hallway. Susan looked behind us and I saw the color drain from her face. I turned my head; I couldn't see the front doors. "It's just not well lit," I said quietly.

She swallowed visibly. "Uh huh."

"Here we are," the Guide said, forcing our attention back to whatever was ahead of us. He gestured towards a large door. It looked like it was made out of mahogany, but I wasn't sure. "Now, are you ready for a rare experience?"

"How rare?" Susan asked. I could tell she was trying to sound light and breezy, but her voice was shaking.

"Rare enough," the Guide said with a small smile.

"Sure," I replied before Susan could say no. "It's a vacation, after all."

"For some," the Guide said as he turned and pushed the door inward. I noticed there was no doorknob or handle.

He ushered us into the room ahead of him. It was smaller than I was expecting after the hallway – more like a large parlor you'd see in an English countryside-type movie. There were sofas and chairs, coffee tables, a couple of tea carts complete with doilies and tea sets, sofa tables behind the larger couches, lamps, rugs, throws and pillows. The room was well lit and there were three other couples in it. I could feel Susan relax.

A small nondescript man came and took our bags. "Please, sit," the Guide said, indicating an open loveseat. Susan gave the small man her cosmetics case and sank into her seat. I sat down next to her and put my arm around her shoulders. She snuggled next to me and I felt her breathing return to normal.

"Now that you're all here, the festivities can begin," the Guide said with a brief smile.

I looked around at the others in the room. No one was familiar-looking to me, but I'd expected that. We all knew each other by reputation, but it was a rarity to be up for promotion at the same time as another employee you knew well. I could tell who were the boss' employees, though – they were the ones who looked calm and confident. Like Susan, their companions looked relieved and confused.

"What festivities?" a rather dumpy woman of what I guessed were middle years asked. She was clearly the companion in her couple – the man with her was about her age but looked more worldly and experienced. He looked Susan up and down appraisingly and she blushed.

"We're playing a game," another woman answered for the Guide. She was younger, probably in her late thirties. She would have been considered a classic beauty in the olden days, which wasn't a surprise. She was still attractive now, though interestingly to me, she wasn't in the best physical shape, tending towards the heavier side of chubby. She had a certain charisma that made me want to ignore this, however, and just focus on her, as it were. I could tell the other men in the room felt the same.

She was easily spotted as the employee in her couple – she was clearly the most confident person in the room, and looking at her gave me the feeling she was that confident with the boss as well.

The man with her was handsome, but he looked the most uncomfortable of anyone in the room. "Honey, you shouldn't interrupt," he said quietly.

She gave him a fond look. "It's one of my strong points, my boss says so all the time." She looked over at the Guide and grinned.

The Guide smiled back. "Yes, Helen, your penchant for taking charge was mentioned in my briefing. You should enjoy the festivities very much, I think."

Another man cleared his throat. He was dressed impeccably, and I could tell everything on him was the finest and most expensive available, down to his sleek leather gloves. He was with a woman many years his junior, dressed all in gold. She was clinging to his arm and looked more uncomfortable than Susan.

"When are things going to get started?" this man asked in a tone that made it clear he wasn't used to waiting.

The Guide gave him a pleasant nod. "Michael, I know you don't approve of time-wasting. However, there are certain...formalities that must be observed. As you are well aware."

Everyone nodded. The Guide gave us all a close-lipped smile. "Excellent. Now, your luggage will be taken to your rooms. Before dinner, a little game has been proposed."

"A game?" the woman in gold asked. "But I'd like to freshen up first."

The Guide shook his head. "Things must go in order. Don't worry – you'll have plenty of time later."

"Time for what?" Susan whispered to me.

I hugged her but didn't answer.

The Guide pointed to a door opposite the one we'd entered through. "This door leads to another room. In that room are three doors. Choose a door, choose a path."

The handsome man with Helen cocked his head. "You're sending us on some sort of hunt?"

The Guide nodded. "A treasure hunt. Of a kind. You may stay together in a group or divide up however you see fit."

"Well, that's chummy," the worldly looking man said.

The Guide chuckled. "Yes, Johnny, I knew you'd find it so." He opened his hands. "If you look well, you'll find maps along the way."

"Maps?" Susan asked. "Why would we need maps?"

Helen laughed. "It's a maze." All the companions stared at her, varying degrees of shock in their expressions. "It's fun," she said with another laugh. "Come on, let's go." She got up and led the way. The rest of us followed.

The room with the doors was smaller than the parlor. It fit the eight of us just fine, but we couldn't have easily added in anyone else.

"Why is it so murky in here?" Susan murmured to me. "Can't your boss afford lighting?"

"Why do we have to do this?" the handsome man with Helen asked.

"Rules," Michael said with authority. "It's how things are done here."

"Where is 'here' exactly?" Susan asked.

The other employees gave me looks that said my companion was asking the smart questions. Helen looked impressed, Johnny looked interested in Susan in a sexual way, and Michael looked annoyed and impatient. I was glad I hadn't run into Michael before – he wasn't my kind of guy.

I hugged Susan. "We're at the start of the maze."

"Right, first decision point," Helen said cheerfully as we all stared at the three doors in front of us. "Who's going where?"

"You know, we haven't even been introduced," her companion said. He wasn't wrong, even though I'd figured out who the other employees were already, and I was sure they'd figured out who I was, too. We'd been late, so the Guide had probably dropped hints before we arrived. "We're Helen and William Troyan-McMichael."

I had no reason to hide. "I'm Matt Spear and this is my wife, Susan."

Michael sighed. "Michael King, and this is my wife, Oriana."

"John and Carla Nova," Johnny said with a grin. "You can call me the luckiest man in the world, by the way."

"Why is that?" Oriana asked politely.

Johnny hugged his wife. "I convinced this lady to

marry me."

Carla smiled. "It didn't take much convincing. Besides, I'm the lucky one to have finally found a man who loves me for myself."

I took this to mean that Carla was an heiress of some kind. It would fit Johnny's reputation as the ladies' man of all ladies' men. Carla was certainly nothing much to look at and she was outshone by the other three women in terms of personality, too. None of the other women had a chance against Helen's natural charisma, of course, but Susan was both beautiful and personable, or else I wouldn't have married her, and even acting like a scared mouse, Oriana had more sex appeal than Carla.

"Sweet," Michael said in a tone indicating he found sweet to be nauseating. "Let's get going, shall we?"

"I think we should stick together," Oriana said nervously.

"Nonsense," Michael said. "Good luck to all of you." He took Oriana's hand and led her through the right-hand door.

"Maybe we should follow him," Johnny said with a laugh. "He always seems to make the right choices."

Helen shrugged. "Why not?"

"Why don't we choose to go back?" Susan asked. She pulled me back to the door that led back to the parlor. Susan pushed against it and gasped. "It won't open! And there's no door handle." She looked at me, eyes wild. "Matt, what's going on?"

I put my arm around her shoulders and drew her back to the doors, so I was next to Helen. "It's just the boss' way of having a joke on us."

"All part of the game," Helen added. "Really,

Susan, honey, you need to relax. It's all in fun. Matt's been around the block more than once. He'll take care of you." She smiled at me, a very knowing smile. "In one way or another," she added softly, where no one else could hear.

"So," Johnny said a little more loudly than necessary. "Are we going to follow Michael, stick together and choose another door, or all split up?"

A bloodcurdling scream answered him.

"It came from the way Michael and Oriana went!" Carla shouted.

"No, from the middle," William said.

"I heard it from the left," Susan said to me. "What do we do?"

"I don't want to split up," William said. "There's safety in numbers.

A throat cleared behind us. We all turned. Susan jumped, but I was still holding her, so I was able to control her somewhat.

The Guide was standing there. "I must insist that the rest of you begin the festivities."

"How did you get in here?" Susan asked, her voice trembling.

The Guide chuckled. "The same way you did." He strode past us and went through the right-hand door.

"So, he'll handle Michael and Oriana if they were in trouble," Helen said.

"What if the person who screamed wasn't one of them?" Susan asked. She was definitely asking the right questions.

"I don't trust that man to help anyone," Carla said flatly. Interesting. "Let's go see if we can help." She grabbed Johnny's hand and pulled him through the right-hand door.

"Joining them or joining us?" Helen asked. "It would be nice to get to know you better, Matt. And Susan."

Susan eyed Helen up and down. For the first time since coming she didn't seem frightened or nervous. "I think we'll try it alone." Susan looked up at me. "Middle or left?"

"You know me, I like the straight and narrow."

"Left for us then," Helen said cheerfully. "See you on the other side." She took William's hand and led him through, even as he protested that we should all continue to stick together.

My arm was still around Susan's shoulders. "Ready?"

She took a deep breath. "No. But let's do this anyway." She shoved the middle door open and we walked through.

"Great," Susan groaned. "Another creepy hallway. Seriously, does your insane boss have a problem with actually using electricity?"

"No. I'm sure it's just done like this for ambiance."

We walked down the hall hand-in-hand. There were doors along this hallway. Susan had us try every one. None of them opened. "Less choices," she said as we reached the end of the hallway where a last door sat. "Thank God for that." She tried this door. Like the others, it didn't budge. "Oh, are you kidding me?"

I tried the door too. "Maybe we have to go back and go through the right or left sides."

Susan sighed and we walked back. She had us try all the doors again. "Just in case." But all the doors stayed firmly shut.

I'd heard sounds behind each door, but since Susan hadn't mentioned it, I didn't bring it up. Why tell her I heard faint scratching or panting behind the doors we couldn't get inside? It would only make her more nervous.

We reached the other end of the hallway. Susan opened the door. "Well, at least this one opens both ways." We stepped through and she gave a little scream.

The room wasn't the one we'd left. It was hard to call it a room. It was a lot easier to call it a countryside.

"This isn't where we just left. Matt, how did we get outside?"

"We're not outside." I pointed up. "The ceiling's painted to look like we're outside, but it's still a ceiling. Look, the birds don't move."

"There had better be some kind of amazing banquet waiting for us when we finish this thing. Either that, or you need to change jobs."

"You know I love what I do, hon. It'll be fine."

"Will it?" Susan looked around. "All I see are trees and hills and things like that."

"It's a room. It's painted to give the illusion of space and depth. We'll go along the wall and that way we'll find a door out of here. It's that, or we go back into the hallway again."

Susan looked behind us. "Let's just see if we *can*."

She opened the door. Sure enough, the dimly lit hallway was on the other side. "Okay, that so-called exit is still there. So, I guess we have that option if your idea doesn't work." She left the door open. I didn't close it. It wouldn't matter.

Another scream echoed. It sounded farther away than the first one had. "Should we investigate?"

"I guess so." Susan shook herself. "I can relate to whoever's screaming their head off, so let's see if we can help them. I think William was right – we should have all stuck together."

I put my hand onto the wall and we walked on. The screaming was replaced with the sound of someone sobbing. This sound was close, though.

Susan pulled out of my hand and went to our left, towards a nearby hillock. I lost sight of her for a moment and decided I'd better go after her. We could find the wall, and the other exit in this room, in a bit.

Happily, she hadn't gone far. The sound of sobbing was louder. "It's coming from here, right here," Susan said. "But there's no one but us."

"Let's go. I'm starting to get as creeped out as you are."

She shook her head and stared at the hillock. "You know, this is really small, barely seven feet tall and only a few feet wide. Do you think…could someone be trapped inside it."

"Oh, I'm sure not." I took her hand and dragged her away. The sobbing got softer the more steps we took. "Let's get out of here."

"Matt, I really think someone was in that little hill."

"I doubt it." I made sure Susan couldn't see my face. She might be able to tell that I knew exactly who was in that hillock. Well, not exactly. But not everyone who visited the boss' estates came to receive a promotion. And failure to complete the maze wasn't met with a congratulatory handshake or a slap on the back.

"This is, officially, the worst trip we've ever taken."

"Maybe it'll get better. You used to like haunted houses."

"Because you'd hold me when I was scared."

I grinned and pulled her closer to me. "Then I'll hold you again now." I wrapped my arm around her shoulders again. She liked it and it made it easier for me to keep her focused on going forward, not back. There was a tree in front of us, but I was pretty sure it was painted on the wall, just painted really well. "Look, I think that's a door."

Susan stared at the tree. "Maybe. Is that knothole the doorknob?"

"You really are the smartest woman, you know that?"

She smiled at me and reached for it. It turned and we both breathed a sigh of relief as the door opened.

The room we entered looked like a storage closet, albeit a large one. "Really?" Susan said. "Oh well, I guess it's better than hills that cry."

"True enough." I hoped she wouldn't ask to look inside the boxes.

"You know, that Guide said we'd find maps if we looked. I didn't think to do it before, but do you think there's a map hidden here somewhere?"

I reached over to the box nearest me. "Not hidden." I handed her the map.

"Oh, wow. That's great!" Susan opened it eagerly. She was back to feeling like she had a handle on the situation. Good.

She didn't have time to read it, however, because another scream sounded. This one was followed by a lot of laughter and applause.

"Who sees or hears someone scream and then laughs and claps?" Susan sounded annoyed, which was better than nervous or scared. Having the map in hand really did wonders for her state of mind.

"Maybe there's a show going on. It would explain all the weird things we've heard."

"You mean like we'll get to the end of this maze and there will be a play for us to watch, like a reward for putting up with this craziness?"

"Yeah, something like that."

"I'd like to see that, Matt, I really would." Susan looked around. "You know, I only see one door in this room, the one we came through."

I opened it. The outdoors room was on the other side. "You want to go back in there?"

"Never again if I can help it." Susan consulted her map. "I think that room is the Conservatory. I didn't see a lot of plants but it fits, size-wise, and I don't see any other rooms listed."

"Listed? What kind of map is that?"

"The less than helpful kind. It lists the rooms, and how many doors are in them, and which room each door leads to. So, the Conservatory had a lot of doors, lucky us. However..."

"However?"

"There's one called Storage. That's clearly where we are. So, Storage has two doors. One that leads to the Conservatory and one that leads to...the Stage."

"See? Maybe I'm right. Let's keep on looking. Maybe we can get to the play before it's all over."

We tapped on all the walls, but none of them sounded hollow and there were no doors. Susan looked up. "I don't see anything on this ceiling, but do you think we're supposed to knock through it?"

"Maybe. Let's move these boxes first, just in case."

We started lifting and shoving. "They're light, at least." Susan shoved a set of boxes out of the way. One fell. It remained closed, thankfully. She stamped on the ground. "Nothing."

"Why is there a little rug here?" I moved the boxes off the patch of carpet and Susan pulled it up.

"Jackpot!" There was a trapdoor.

I pulled it up. It was very dark inside. Blacker than black dark. The kind of dark that says you're never going to see light again. There was also a stepladder leading down. It wouldn't let two go side-by-side.

Susan gulped. "You first or me?"

"Me. I'm the man, you're my wife. Just follow right after me, and don't step on my fingers."

She gave a shaky laugh, folded the map up, and tucked it into her bosom. I started down. Once my head was all she could see, Susan got onto the ladder, too.

We were in total blackness. The trapdoor was still open, but it seemed farther away than it should, like a tiny patch of light we'd never reach again. "Matt? You still there?" Susan whispered.

"Yeah. Haven't hit bottom yet."

We went down ninety-nine steps by my count. I'd

been expecting thirty-three, but the boss liked to have his jokes. Next time I did this, it might be a hundred and thirty-two or even a hundred and ninety-eight. One set of thirty-three for each millennia.

Finally my foot hit what felt like floor. "I think we're there. Hang on, let me be sure."

"Don't let go of the ladder!"

"I won't." With one hand holding tight to the side of the ladder, I felt around with my foot. There was certainly enough room for two to stand here. "Come on down."

I kept my hand out so I could feel her when she reached the floor. As she stepped off the last rung of the ladder, I pulled her to me. "I can't tell what else is in here." I wrapped my arm around her again. "I think we want to move slowly and stay close together."

I wasn't happy with our location. This was a game, but it was also a test, and any one of us could fail. If I'd have had a choice, I'd have gone back to the Conservatory rather than down in here, but I'd have had to give Susan an explanation and that wasn't in the rules of the game. Besides, any explanation I could give would only terrify her more, not less.

"No argument from me, Matt. At all." Susan put her arm around my waist. She was shivering.

Now that we were together I could let go of the ladder and touch the wall. We inched along it to our right, and I tested every step carefully. I'd never been in this room before, but I'd heard the rumors. In this room, one wrong step and we'd spend the rest of existence in this darkness, only we wouldn't be together.

My left foot slipped, just a little, and I shoved us

both closer to the wall. I took a deep breath and kept moving, even more slowly. After what seemed like an eternity, I felt an opening. There was still floor, but no more wall.

We rounded this corner in the same way – inching our way. Happily it was a corner, not a drop off into nothingness.

"Do you see something?" Susan asked. "Like a little white fluttering, way off in the distance?"

"Maybe."

We got closer. Susan was right, there was definitely something small and white fluttering in front of us, though it was still far off. Susan tried to hurry, but I held her tightly. Just because we could see an exit didn't mean we could reach it.

It took a few more minutes, and then we were in light. Like the hallways we'd been in, it wasn't a lot of light, but after the total darkness it seemed bright. There was a curtain in front of us.

We looked at each other. Susan shrugged. We pushed the curtain aside.

The stage we stepped out on was empty. Well, empty of people. There were a lot of props hanging from the catwalks.

"Are those supposed to be angels, devils, and demons?" Susan asked as she looked around.

"Looks like it. So much for our play idea, though." The seating was a half-and-half, where the main aisle went down the middle of the room and aligned with the middle of the stage. There were plenty of seats, but no one was in them. "It's a weird setup anyway. Who has their theater aisle in the middle?"

"It's not pitch black, I'm okay with it." Susan sat down at the edge of the stage and pulled out her map. "Okay, the Stage has two other doors. One leads to the Conservatory. That's a popular spot."

"Well, you said it had a lot of doors."

"True. The other leads to, get this, the Maze."

"I thought we were in the maze."

"Me too, but I guess it's an official maze." Susan looked at me. "I think I hate your boss."

I shrugged. "He's eccentric, I'll give you that."

She looked around the room. "I don't want to go back to the Conservatory, and I don't want to go back into total darkness."

"I only see one door." I pointed to the other end of the room. The single door lined up with the center aisle.

"That means the other door is hidden. And I'll bet it's another walk in the darkness. Let's take the one in front of us, regardless of where it leads."

I jumped down off the stage and lifted her off by her waist. Susan giggled and I kissed her. "See? We can have fun even in the middle of a weird maze."

She hugged me. "True enough."

We were about to walk up the aisle when we heard voices. "I think they're coming from behind the curtain, the other side from where we came."

"At least they're not screaming or crying."

They were arguing. "I told you, stop worrying, stop crying, stop whining." I didn't need to see him to recognize the voice – it was Michael.

He strode on stage, Oriana stumbling behind him. He wasn't holding onto her. Her face was streaked with tears and her hair was a mess.

"Oh, you're here," Michael said. "Where did you come from?"

"Storage," Susan said. "Via a really long, dark, horrible path."

"Us too," Oriana said, sniffling. "But we weren't in a storage room."

"Were you the one screaming earlier?" Susan asked.

Oriana shook her head. "I was too scared to scream. I hate this place."

"Some people would appreciate this kind of entertainment being created specifically for them," Michael said.

"Who in the hell would that be?" Carla asked as she came out from behind the curtain, Johnny right behind her. "This is the craziest place I've ever been, and I've been all over the world."

"She's a little freaked out," Johnny said. "Sorry."

"Who can blame her?" Oriana muttered.

"Were you all in the Conservatory?" Susan asked.

"Yes," Michael replied.

"If you mean that weird looks like it's open air but isn't place with the crying hills, yes," Carla answered.

"You're reading the map right, hon," I said quietly. "Not that I ever had a doubt."

Susan smiled proudly. "Then let's head for the Maze."

"We're *in* the maze," Michael said with disdain. I really didn't like him.

"No," I said before Susan could reply. "This is a special maze within the larger maze. We have a map."

Michael rolled his eyes, but he got down off the

stage. Johnny jumped down like I had and helped Carla. Then he helped Oriana. Carla didn't seem to care. Probably because she was freaked out. Apparently when she was freaked out Carla got angry.

We walked up the aisle. As we reached the door Susan pointed. "Look." There was a folder bin attached to the wall with "MAPS" emblazoned on it. Susan took one.

"We have a map," I pointed out.

She opened it. "Oooh, this is a different map. This one is for the Maze specifically."

The other women grabbed copies as well.

Thusly armed, I opened the door and we all stepped through.

"More doors," Carla said flatly. "Goody."

"Not really doors," Johnny said. "More like openings."

I agreed with him – there were four openings in front of us, but none had an actual door. The two on either side turned immediately right or left, depending. The two in the middle went farther in, then one turned right and the other left.

The room was large; it felt larger than the Conservatory. The maze walls were high, close to the ceiling. There was no way to get over a wall. The walls looked solid; there was probably no way to break through one, either.

"Maze starting points." Susan was reading the new map, old map tucked back into her bosom. "This is set up like a real English hedge maze. The map has it all laid out. This should be fun, actually."

I refrained from mentioning what could hide in a giant hedge.

"Fun is going to a lovely day spa," Oriana said. "Not this."

"Maybe there will be a spa at the end," Susan said encouragingly.

"Maybe there will be more maze crap at the end," Carla said. She heaved a sigh. "But, as far as I can tell, we're stuck going through this."

"I'm hungry," Oriana said quietly. "And thirsty."

The rest of us, now that it was mentioned, shared that we could use some food and water, too. But there wasn't any.

"I say again, some host," Carla snapped. "This is the prettiest looking dump I've ever had the displeasure of visiting."

Johnny shrugged. "Let's look for the way out, and then maybe there will be a sumptuous feast and wine aplenty when we exit."

Oriana managed a little smile. Carla snorted. Johnny shook his head, but offered an arm to each of them. "Ladies, shall we?"

"Michael?" Oriana asked timidly.

He rolled his eyes. "Fine, we'll travel along with them for a while." Oriana grabbed Johnny's arm quickly. After her trip through the dark without Michael holding onto her, I couldn't blame her.

"We'll go it alone," I said quickly.

"You're sure?" Johnny sounded disappointed.

"Positive." I could have stood spending time with Johnny and Oriana. But Carla was close to dancing on my last nerve and it had been a long time since I'd wanted to hit someone as much as I wanted to punch Michael in the face. And there was no way any employee would allow themselves to be separated from their companion. Not here.

The others grumbled for a bit, then Carla, who was looking at her map, chose a direction and they headed off. We could hear them bickering for quite a while.

"You don't work with Michael, do you?" Susan, who was still studying our map, asked.

"No. Thankfully."

"Yeah, I don't like him much, either. You know, Matt, this maze doesn't seem to actually have an end. I think it's more like a…trap."

"Oh, if you work at it, you'll find your way out." The voice came from behind us. Even though I recognized it, I jumped just like Susan did.

We turned to see the Guide standing there. "Is it possible to get some water or a snack?" Susan asked. "We've been doing this so-called game for hours."

"It hasn't been as long as it seems to you," the Guide said. "Time has a way of…getting tangled up in mazes."

"I'll bet." Susan sighed. "Water? Any chance of that?"

The Guide frowned. "I'm sorry, but there is no food or beverage allowed inside the maze."

"Of course there isn't." Susan shook herself. "Now I sound like Carla. Okay, fine. Any suggestions for how we get out of this or the best way to go? Based on this map, there are destination points, but none of them lead to an actual exit."

"There are doorways of all kinds in here," the Guide said as he turned away. "Each find their own."

Carla and her group had gone through the leftmost entrance. The Guide went through the middle-right one.

"So, middle left or far right?" I asked Susan.

She grimaced. "Not sure really. I kind of wish I knew which way Helen and William picked."

"What makes you think they were here already?"

"No idea. You're right. For all we know, they went a different way completely and are nowhere near here."

"I wish," William said as he and Helen walked out of the middle-left path. "Dead end at every turn." He sighed. "Honey, do we have to go back in?"

"The Stage is behind us," Susan said. "But I think the paths out of it are both pretty horrible."

Helen laughed. It was a tinkling sound most women couldn't manage but all women tried for. A laugh that went right into a man's gut and twirled around and down into his groin. "Oh, William, we'll be just fine."

"I don't want to take you on some horrible path," he said protectively. "Maybe we should go back in there."

Helen smiled. "Let's rest here for a bit and then decide."

"No water or food," Susan said.

"We'll make do, honey," Helen replied. "I'd try the right-most path. Maybe it'll be good for you."

I took Susan's hand. "Thanks for the tip."

"See you on the other side," Helen called as we entered the Maze.

This path was fairly simple to follow for quite a while. We turned frequently, enough that it was hard to remember which was the way we were supposedly heading. But it was all turns, no forks, no decisions.

Of course, it couldn't last. We finally came to a three-way intersection. "Right, left, or straight?" I asked Susan, who had kept track of every step on her map.

"Straight. I think. The map shows that they all lead back on each other."

"One way's as good as another if it all leads to nowhere."

"So true, Mister Philosopher."

We were instantly faced with turn options. We headed back and checked the other two paths – both also had intersections almost immediately.

"None of these show on the map," Susan said worriedly.

"Then we just give it a shot and see where we end up."

We went back to the middle path and started picking directions at random. I'd pick one, then Susan, then me, and so on. The intersections were random – sometimes we'd walk a few paces and hit a new intersection, other times we'd go for a good few yards before we had to choose where to turn.

We were moving quickly, and moved faster as we went on. Not out of excitement or even impatience. There were noises coming from behind many of the walls. Snarling, sobbing, scratching, moaning. Some of the noises sounded human. Some didn't.

"This place is horrible," Susan said. "I don't see any way that the sounds could be piped in from anywhere else other than inside the walls."

We knocked on the walls, but no one knocked back. In some cases, our knocking made the noises go away. In others, the noises got louder. And sounded closer.

"Do you think there are animals or people in here making those noises?" Susan asked.

"No idea," I lied. Well, I knew they weren't animals as she'd know them. Or people, either.

The third time that happened we both started to trot. We rounded a corner to find another intersection. "Is this the twentieth?" Susan asked.

"I've lost count. My turn to pick?"

"Yeah."

"Left." We turned, still at a trot. But we both pulled up and stopped dead. "A door?"

"Maybe it's an exit," Susan said excitedly. She grabbed the handle.

"Wait a second –"

Scrabbling and scratching interrupted me. It was loud, insistent, desperate. Susan let go of the door and backed away. The scratching continued and increased.

"Do we go in?" Susan asked in a whisper. The scrabbling became frenzied. And the door moved just a bit.

"No way." I had a good guess what was behind this door, and it wasn't something anyone would want to meet. There were plenty of ways to lose your promotion, and being ripped apart by an unnamed monster from the depths was certainly one of them. I grabbed her hand. "We run."

We turned and ran. I could have sworn I heard a door slam behind us. I hoped it was slamming closed, not open, but wasn't willing to bet on that kind of luck. We sped up, flinging ourselves down paths willy-nilly.

I heard scratching for a long time.

The sound finally died down as we rounded another corner and hit a dead end. We spun and ran back, choosing a different path. Dead end again.

Well, dead end with a door. This time, Susan only touched the knob, she didn't turn it. Scratching ensued. We turned and ran like hell.

I lost count of how many turns we made, how many dead ends we hit, and how many doors we reached that all had the same creepy scratching coming from behind them – but it was a lot.

We ran on, and this time we were rewarded with a long hall. It had a lot of paths jutting off it, but we ran to the end. The hall turned to the right, and we went with it. To find another dead end.

"Now what?" Susan asked.

I leaned against the wall to catch my breath. "Now we figure out how to get out of here without going near any of those doors ever again."

"Three paces down, then we turn right." Susan bit her lip. "I think."

The hall had turned out to be a decent choice. Susan had been able to identify where we were because of it, and now we were trying to get out of this section as fast as we could without doing any more blind panic runs that would lead us to scary doors with scarier sounds coming from behind them.

"It's okay," I replied. "At least we're away from those doors and those awful noises. Whatever they were."

"It sounded like badgers," she said. "At least, some of them did."

"Badgers? I thought they all sounded like claws scrabbling against the walls. Long, sharp and nasty claws."

"Some sounded like badgers to me," Susan replied, as we turned walked two more paces and faced another dead end. "Sorry," she said miserably. "I really thought I'd counted right."

"The clawing would've made anyone mess up. Let's face it, that you even have a guess as to where we are after the last section we were in is a credit to your brains and map-reading skills and nothing else."

"Thanks. I'd feel a whole lot smarter if I could get us out of here."

I looked around. The walls weren't any lower, still high enough that we couldn't see the ceiling clearly. "Any hidden doors?" Not that the doors around here, hidden or otherwise, sounded like a good bet.

Susan tapped. "Nothing I can detect. Matt, how are we going to get out of here?"

"The Guide said that if we worked at it, we'd find our way."

"What a great vacation." Susan sounded on the verge of tears. "We've been in here for days." We hadn't been, not in reality, but I had to admit it felt like it by now.

I shrugged. "I thought it was weird, but you know, when the boss sends you on an all-expenses paid vacation, you don't argue."

"Guess we should have."

"Let's go back and see if we can make any sort of progress."

We retraced our steps. "Okay, let's go to the left here," Susan said with sudden authority. I thought I saw something small and white fluttering up ahead. She headed right toward it. She was moving fast, almost as fast as she'd been when we'd been running away from the whatevers behind the doors, and I had to trot to keep up with her.

Susan reached another intersection, turned right without seeming to think about it, left at the next three intersections, then right again. I could see the fluttering thing just ahead of us the whole way. I was fairly sure she was following it. I chose not to mention that the fluttering thing hadn't exactly helped us the last time we'd seen it because, well, maybe it had and I didn't realize it.

We walked through an archway and were in a large garden. Lots of flowers, shrubs and trees lined the far edges, creating their own kind of walls. They were grown so thick there was no way to get through. There was plenty of space in here, though – the only overgrowth was along the edges.

There was a small hillock in the very center of all of this, and on it stood one tree. The tree had fruit hanging from its limbs and the white fluttering thing flying around it. There was a small wrought iron fence around the base of the hillock. The fence was clearly there for show – a child could climb over it easily.

This was the moment of truth. Susan was smart, beautiful, and loved me. If I refused the promotion right now, the boss would understand. I'd be up for another promotion soon enough, after all, because I really was that good. The only rule about promotions the boss had, other than surviving the Test of Worth, was that you couldn't refuse promotion three times in a row. This was the first promotion I'd even considered passing on in a very long time, so I definitely had the leeway.

We'd have to actually get out of the maze unscathed, but that was a doable thing. I knew for a fact that Helen ran the maze all the time, simply because she enjoyed the challenge. She was legendary, even among the boss' employees, and she remained one of his favorites, so my following suit wouldn't go against me in any way.

These facts made my decision harder.

I took Susan's hand. "Another dead end. Let's try it again."

Susan shook her head, not looking at me. "No. I want to see that tree." She pulled her hand out of mine and moved closer to it, then crawled over the fence.

"Not a good idea. Remember the last time a woman messed around with a tree?"

"Yeah. They got kicked out of a garden." She turned to me, and her eyes looked wild. "I want out of here, Matt. I want out now."

"I love you."

"I love you, too. And I want us to get out of here and go home." With that, she reached up and grabbed a piece of fruit hanging from the laden branches, twisted its stem, pulled it off and bit into it, all within three seconds.

I watched her chew and swallow. She was about to take another bite when her eyes bulged. I could tell she couldn't breathe, and it wasn't long before her face actually turned blue, and then black. She keeled over, right there.

The apple fell from her hand and rolled next to the fence. I saw two others just like it. Not three others, though.

I wondered who'd chosen to stay with their current position instead of choosing advancement. Maybe Helen. She'd been around a long time, after all, even before she launched those thousand ships, and could easily wait for another opportunity. And perhaps William had listened to her when they'd reached the Garden. Or maybe Helen had insisted.

I was certain Johnny was ready to trade up, regardless of career advancement – his reputation wasn't built on being the best lover of one woman, but every woman. Plus he was going to inherit a fortune. Win-win for the greatest lover in the world all the way around.

Michael, well, when everything you touch turns to gold, you can get as many sweet young things as you want. Oriana was undoubtedly gone.

I heard a step behind me. "Would you like to take your bow? The audience loved your performance."

"Not really, if it's all the same to you." I didn't turn around. Some things you just didn't do. Maybe Helen looked right at the boss' face, but I wasn't that sort of risk-taker.

"Of course. I never force anyone to do something they don't want to. I thought for a few moments that you might have chosen to stay at your current position. For a little longer at any rate."

"I considered it."

"But you didn't press for it."

"No."

No, I hadn't pressed for it. The decision I'd made weeks ago, when I'd been advised it was promotion time, was still the right one. If Susan had listened to me and left the Garden, then I'd have willingly changed my mind. But she'd wanted out, and now, she was out. One way or another.

"No regrets?"

I thought about it. It was never wise to not think about your answer when speaking with the boss. "Not really, no. I loved her, we had a good life together. But nothing lasts forever."

"Except for a select few, that is true."

"That's why we work for you. May I go now?" I asked politely.

"Yes. You have fulfilled your part of the bargain. One beloved soul given to me in exchange for wealth, health and longevity."

"Old School divorce, New School benefits. Adam should have paid better attention to the snake. Thanks, boss."

He chuckled. "Thank *you*, Methuselah."

The trees at the far end of the garden moved apart. I could see my car in the parking lot. I walked to it without looking back.

After all, finding another wife is easy, but living forever takes real planning.

The
Disciple

THE DISCIPLE

I wasn't always alone.

Before this time I had two families, one related by blood, the other by purpose. But they're all gone now. I used to hope I'd see them again, in Heaven, if nowhere else, but now I know that will never be.

Of course, my calling has always been a lonely one. Sent back in time to stop the most virulent plague to ever hit mankind. Sent back in time to prevent the horrifying future, but never to return to it.

Seven of us were sent back to the Middle Ages, trained to adapt and survive in a world more different from our own than a twenty-fourth century mind could imagine. But for all the changes, some things were the same.

In the mid-twenty-fourth century, the world came to the realization all those vampire "myths" were, in fact, real. As real as death, but less kind.

I don't know how the vampires began, whether the church legends are true, or if the Romanian ones are more accurate. All I know is that vampires originally drank the blood of animals and their own family groups, but as time and technology progressed they learned how to live off of others not blood-related.

Human blood is tastier than animal, apparently, and by the time I was born, vampires were the biggest threat humanity had ever seen.

They were the biggest threat my family would ever know.

I was seventeen when my family was captured by a 'Pire gang. Not to be turned – for food. I was forced to watch, held and kept helpless by a laughing vampire. "Stop struggling," he whispered in my ear. "Behave, and maybe I'll turn you, or keep you as my thrall."

The leaders drank their fill, then tossed my parents to the rest of their gang. They drained my mother and father alive. When I sleep, I can still hear their screams, the last sounds my parents ever made.

Then they tasted my grandparents. "Not fresh," the male leader sneered as he crushed my grandmother's head between his hands. His mate did the same with my grandfather.

They turned on me and my little sister next.

"These will be sweet," the leader's mate said.

"Sissy," Violet said as tears streamed down her face. "I'm scared."

"Let my sister go," I begged, even though I knew it was pointless. "You can do whatever you want with me, but let her live."

The 'Pire holding me laughed. "We can do whatever we want with you anyway."

The 'Pire leader grabbed Violet. He smiled at me. "I think we'll keep this little one. She can feed off of her brave big sister as her first meal." With that, he sank his fangs into Violet's neck.

Violet's skin drained of color until she looked like marble. But her chest still moved, so I knew she was breathing. "Fight it," I called to her. "Don't let them turn you."

The vampire holding me laughed and whispered in

my ear again. "There is no fighting it. Once bitten, you're ours for eternity."

"You like that one?" the leader's mate asked my vampire.

"I do."

She shrugged. "Then turn her. We can use new pets."

I struggled, but I had no real hope. I prayed to a God I wasn't sure cared about anyone on Earth any more – the last act of the desperate and doomed.

God listened.

The door slammed open and my saviors burst in. The Order, the only ones brave enough to fight back against the 'Pires, ran in. Their holy symbols jingled, a beautiful sound, as they sprayed holy water and golden bullets out of their machine guns.

The 'Pires dropped Violet and me to face the real threat. I crawled to her and cradled her in my arms. "Hang on, baby girl," I whispered. "Don't leave Sissy all alone."

Her eyes fluttered open. "So cold."

"I know." I hugged her to me as a big man picked us both up and carried us away from the carnage. I watched The Order kill every 'Pire. When I'm sad, I close my eyes, and I can still hear their screams, the most beautiful sound in the world.

Three of the women doused all the remains with gasoline – my family's and the 'Pires' alike – and lit the bodies with a blowtorch. My last view of my family was this obscene funeral pyre.

I was saved, but Violet wasn't so lucky. The vampire's bite had infected her remaining blood. We watched, back at the safe house, as she began to change.

She lay on a wooden table, bound at the waist. She remained pale, dead-looking. She was still breathing, but it was shallow. Her eyes opened and they weren't human eyes any more. The pupils were too large and the look in them was too bestial.

"Can't she fight it? Can't we stop it somehow?" I was begging and again I knew it was fruitless.

Armand, the Head of The Order, shook his head sadly. "I've only heard of a few over the ages who could fight the infection. It's too late." He was a big, muscular man, with chocolate skin, wild curly hair, and a full beard. I saw sorrow in his kind, brown eyes and knew he was telling the truth. With that confirmation came the knowledge of what had to be done, what I had to do.

Violet looked at me and smiled. "Come give baby girl a hug." Her voice was wrong – too deep, too seductive.

I picked up a golden stake and went to her. But not too close. "I'm here."

Violet smiled wider. Her eyeteeth elongated. "Come give baby girl a hug," she said more strongly.

"I love you," I said quietly.

She lunged towards me, mouth opened, fangs gleaming. I'd been expecting it. I slammed the stake into her heart, with so much strength it forced her back and pinned her to the table, like an obscene butterfly I'd collected.

I knew without asking that I hadn't had to be the one who did this. One of the others would have exterminated the threat without issue. One of the others would have taken the last of my little sister's life. But my sister was already gone, and the only way to save her was to kill her.

"Goodbye, Violet." I refused to cry, though I wanted to.

Her eyes changed, just before death. "Bye, Sissy," she said in her own voice. She smiled, then her face froze in the way the faces of the dead do. I try not to see that image every time I close my eyes. I never succeed.

I carried her body into the sunlight. Armand poured holy water over her. I held Violet's body as it burned away and turned to ash, until there was nothing left of my little sister, my family, but dust.

Armand put his hand onto my shoulder. "You'll meet her again. In Heaven, if nowhere else."

"Not in Hell?"

"No. You've already known her in Hell, because Hell is here."

I looked up at him. "I want to destroy them. I want to make this world like it was, not like it is."

Armand nodded, and led me back inside.

I was a member of The Order before they asked me to join.

I was indoctrinated in The Order, taught and trained. I had a new family and we were joined by a different kind of blood – not blood shared but blood spilled.

For two years I learned, studied, worked, and sweated. I wasn't allowed on raids in the first year, but was able to assist in the second. By the end of my apprenticeship, I was ready to join the elite squads.

Killing vampires wasn't what it had been in the old days. Through the years they'd learned how to counter most of the things that had held them in check in the past – sunlight, silver-edged weapons, wooden stakes through the heart. But the Order had done significant research and discovered the keys to confidently eliminating them.

'Pires were indeed affected by religious symbols, but the Star of David was more effective than the Cross of Christ. Combined they were powerful enough to stun and hold any 'Pire near them, whether the vampire could see them or not. Holy water still worked, and could be blessed by any member of any clergy, as long as that person truly believed in their religion. Holy water made a wonderful defensive weapon and worked like acid, at least until the 'Pire regenerated.

What killed them, though, was a combination of metals and woods – iron, silver, ash, and oak – covered in gold. Vampires, it turned out, coveted gold. Any race that lives forever would be drawn to something that never loses its value over time, and through the centuries, this love of gold had become their weakness.

All The Order's weapons were made of this gold-covered mixture. It made the weapons expensive, but the cure for any plague is costly.

The true genius, however, was the invention of the Nightstick.

"You've progressed faster than any other," Armand told me. He was pleased and that meant I was pleased. "Time for you to learn to wield a Nightstick."

I hadn't been allowed a Nightstick yet, and I had to work to contain my excitement. "Thank you."

Armand grinned as he handed me the best weapon The Order had ever produced. "You've earned it."

The Nightstick looked like a large combination wrench and was used in a similar way. One end was rounded, with a hexagonal opening. A Star of David was formed inside the hexagon by thin bars of iron which were covered with silver.

My hand sat between this rounded end and the perpendicular bar forming the Cross of Christ with the main shaft. The other end had U-shaped pinchers.

Armand showed me how the pinchers could open or close as needed, their mechanism housed in the cross-bar.

Like all Nightsticks, mine was made of the woods and metals combination, covered in gold. "It's been blessed by everyone here," Armand said. "Ensure any clergy you meet bless it as well."

"Why?" I asked while I practiced making the pinchers work.

"The more blessings received, the stronger the Nightstick becomes." Armand smiled sadly. "This is our best weapon. It means we have a hope of winning this war."

I knew he was lying to me. The invention of this

weapon made fighting against 'Pires seem possible, but there were so many, legions by the time the Nightstick was perfected, and humanity was thinning quickly.

I smiled back. "I know we can stop them." I lied, but it was a lie I wanted to make a reality.

Weapons technology wasn't the only thing The Order focused on – saving great scientific minds had been a priority from the start, and their "think tank" was impressive. Finally enough great minds were together long enough to come up with the ultimate breakthrough – time travel.

Initial tests – going back an hour, then a day, then a week – worked well, with one drawback. Coming back to present day caused brainwave issues, and the longer the jump, the worse the problems.

Armand called all the operatives together. "We've lost the one-year team," he said without preamble.

"I saw them," Hannah protested. "They looked fine."

Armand shook his head. "Their bodies returned. Their minds didn't."

"We can tell they did what they were supposed to," Liam said. He was alive, which proved the time-travel was working, since he'd been killed twelve months prior. The year-back team's mission had been to save his life.

We'd known their task had been completed because suddenly Liam was with us. The scientists had prepared us, so his reappearance, and its effect on our memories of him – both those that showed he'd died, and those that showed him being with us for the past year – weren't too skewed. We'd all taken a drug that ensured everyone in present time would have no trouble aligning the memories.

Liam had been given the same drug, so he was also able to align his dead self with his now-living self. He could also confirm that the year-back team had come, saved him, then disappeared.

"Yes," Armand said slowly. "The trip back is completely effective, and clearly the operatives retain their present-day memories when they arrive in the past. However, we have to scrap our plans to make short jumps to the past. I've decided to cancel the rest of the short-term jumps because we can't regain the teams."

"Can't we give them the same drug we took?" I asked.

Armand shook his head. "We tried that. It...made their madness worse."

"Why not send the three- and five-year teams back and let them do their work?" Jonathan asked. He was on the five-year team, and clearly disappointed to lose the mission he'd trained for. "Leave us there. We'll catch up."

"It's one thing to go back and return," Liam said. "It's another to go back and stay there."

Armand shook his head. "The tests all agree – the space-time continuum can be negatively affected by leaving the shorter-jump teams in the past for too long."

"Meeting yourself is never a good thing," Marcus said.

Armand nodded. "Yes, exactly. And that's only one of the problems."

"So, we're giving up?" Adrienne asked, sounding appalled.

"No. But..." Armand sighed.

"But?" David asked.

"But if we hope to save humanity today, we must send a team back farther in time. So far back there is no hope of them ever returning."

"This team wouldn't be able to get help, to know if their work was successful," Marcus said. "You go back forever, you live and die in the past?"

"Yes." Armand looked around. "We will be sending the next team back a thousand years. Whoever volunteers will never know if their efforts saved us or not. You'll only be able to do what you can, for as long as you have."

My hand was already in the air. Armand smiled at me. "I knew you would offer. I'm sorry we have to cancel our plans for the three and five year jumps." The three-year team was to have been tasked with saving my family.

"I understand." I did. We needed to save everyone, not just my family. "If I can change the past, then maybe Violet will..." I couldn't finish, couldn't say that maybe if we were successful, then my little sister wouldn't have to die by my hand.

"I'm in," Marcus said, filling the silence my throat tightening had created. He put his arm around my shoulders. "Can't let you be the only risk-taker."

He was tall and handsome, with black hair and sparkling blue eyes. I smiled up at him. "You know I don't need protecting." I liked going on patrols with

Marcus. I liked doing other things with him, too.

Marcus grinned. "Absolutely. I just want to visit the motherland."

Everyone chuckled. "Marcus brings up a good point," Armand said. "We can have only those of clear European descent on this team. Those of us who won't blend in at first sight can't go."

"All races were there at the time," Lin protested. She was Armand's wife, and I knew without asking that she'd hoped the two of them could go back with us. But her Chinese heritage was as clear as his African-American roots.

"Yes," Armand agreed, "but most were in their home countries. The occasional traveler from foreign lands was a rarity, and the less time spent explaining to the locals what the team is doing there, the better."

There were arguments from those operatives whose features would force them to remain in the present. Armand let it go on for a minute or so, the he raised his hand. Everyone quieted.

"We stay here. Not only because we'll stand out, but because our place is to deal with whatever the changes in the past cause in the future – our present. We've made the decision to send a team, we have to be here to deal with the ramifications. That's the fate of leaders, or it should be," he added, looking at Lin.

She nodded slowly. "I agree."

Armand smiled widely. "Besides, won't it be wonderful to discover there are no 'Pires when we wake up the day after the thousand-year-back team leaves?"

Everyone laughed and agreed this would be wonderful. Everyone but those who were busy volunteering for the team. We were discussing other things.

None of us spoke of dying.

Seven was the most that could be sent at one time without risking the travelers being lost in the time-stream. It ended up that the team was made up of three women and four men — me, Marcus, Hannah, David, Liam, Adrienne, and Jonathan. We were all fair skinned with the right looks to be Europeans of the day.

More had volunteered to go, of course. But out of all the volunteers, we were the best trained operatives and had the most 'Pire kills.

"We shouldn't let Liam go," Lin said. "We worked too hard to get him back."

Liam was short and stocky, with a wide grin and a shock of red hair. "Sorry, but I was resurrected for a reason. I'm the medieval scholar, remember? You don't get to keep me here when I'll be more useful there."

Best of the best or not, we trained long and hard, learning every form of martial arts known, becoming experts in a variety of weapons we might come across in our travels, learning about the mores, classes, and expectations of the day.

Our hearing and vision were medically improved – we could hear a whisper a mile away and read the lips of the person sharing the secret. Our bones and teeth were strengthened, our bodies immunized against ancient illnesses as well as modern ones.

Our blood was altered, a dangerous and expensive

process. The taste of garlic, tang of iron, bite of silver, and smell of oak made our blood vile to the 'Pires, which ensured we wouldn't be turned. Because of its new properties, our blood also provided no nourishment to them.

Blood alteration was easier than time travel, but the process was slow and the 'Pires were working fast. If we'd found that serum a decade earlier, maybe we could have immunized the population and scrapped our time-travel plans. Instead, we used it for those in The Order, but, even though our preparations had taken another eighteen months, there was no time for mass distribution.

Once trained and physically prepared, the Far Away Team, as we called ourselves, were outfitted. The Order wanted to ensure we'd be well-equipped – and we were.

We were given two Nightsticks each, two pairs of infrared-heat goggles, medicines and first aid supplies, clothing we hoped would allow us to pass for, if not natives, at least people of the time period, and gold, though not as much of that as we'd have liked.

All our supplies but the Nightsticks stored in carrying bags that were leather on the outside and lined with water-, shock-, heat-, and cold-resistant material that would protect the contents, potentially for centuries.

Everyone had full-body underclothes which were a cloth hybrid that would keep us cool in hot weather and warm in the cold. We all wore leather boots rolled up over our knees, and secured our leather pants with a thick leather belt from which our Nightsticks hung. The belt also "looked" like it was holding our pants up, which allowed us to hide our more modern fastenings.

For protection as well as adornment, we wore leather vests over black shirts. The shirts' color would hide stains and the fact they were a special blend of several layers of silk with gold and silver threaded through the fabric.

Each of us had a cloak as well, made from the same fabric as our shirts, with the addition of a middle layer of the lightest chain mail made of the metals and woods mixture we knew would keep us safe.

Speaking of adornment, we were also given gold and silver jewelry. We wore two necklaces with two charms – the Star of David and the Cross of Christ. One necklace was under shirts, one was worn out, to be seen. We had charm bracelets on each wrist, worn the same as the necklaces – one under our sleeves and hidden by our leather gloves, one worn on the outside.

We were all clergy and well versed in the purification ritual, so holy water wouldn't be a problem. However, we each carried stainless steel vials of it, because it never paid to be without.

The eighteen months passed swiftly, but not fast enough. Humanity's numbers went down while we prepared. By the time we were ready – standing in front of The Order for the last time, dressed in the clothes we'd spend the rest of our lives in – we knew, without a doubt, that we were humanity's last hope.

Armand hugged me. "Be true to your training, your goals, and yourself." He kissed my forehead. "You're like my daughter. I look forward to finding you in the new world you'll create, so I can tell your other self about how you saved us all."

I hugged him back tightly. "I'll make you proud, I

promise."

"I'll take care of her," Marcus said as he hugged Armand. "I'll protect her with my life, I promise."

Armand put his hands to our cheeks. "I hope to see you again, somehow. But we'll meet again in Heaven, if nowhere else."

Finally, all the farewells were said. The seven of us said our last good-bye to everything we'd ever known, stepped onto the platform, and went back in time a thousand years.

We landed in medieval France. Using historical records, the scientists had been able to choose an area that was scarcely populated. We arrived at night, and so were not detected.

It was the best luck we'd have.

We were prepared for anything, we thought. We'd spent months training, being outfitted, readying ourselves. But we weren't prepared for the smell.

Medieval Europe stank to high heaven, especially to our twenty-fourth century noses. Vampires in our time had a scent – old blood and minor decay, mostly – but they were an aromatic treat compared to the average person in this time period.

Luckily, we didn't find any 'Pires for a month, because it took us that long to adjust and begin to ignore the aroma of filth. I would never have guessed that our first challenge would be managing to breath without gagging, but it was.

The Order had chosen this era for a variety of

reasons. Bubonic plague was raging across the land, so any dead bodies we might leave behind or funeral pyres we might have to light would be easily explained. We should be able to wear our protective clothing without causing an issue. And though the languages had changed over the centuries, they were close enough to our native tongues and other languages we'd learned that we could get by. We'd learned Latin as well, in hopes of being able to convince any clergy we might meet to help us in our cause.

But our scientists had also chosen this era because the 'Pire population was reasonably sparse and still restricted to the Eurasian continent. They hadn't needed to migrate to the other continents – possibly hadn't even traveled from Europe into Asia yet. So this was our chance to stop them at the source.

Clearing out an entire continent of vampires sounds easy, when you're looking at ancient maps. We only needed a week to realize the land mass would have been a challenge for seven hundred of us. It was laughable to think the seven of us would manage to make a dent in the problem. Especially when we realized if we wanted to eat, we had to make our meager gold last, which meant we couldn't buy horses.

"Find the pattern," David said, whenever any of us mentioned the seeming futility. "There's always a pattern. We find it, we can trace it back to the source. Find the source, stop the spread."

"What if the pattern leads us thousands of miles?" Jonathan would ask in return.

"Then we walk those miles," was always David's reply.

Because bathing wasn't commonly done, we had to

hide the fact we cleaned ourselves regularly from everyone we encountered, and, despite our European heritages, we already stood out more than we'd hoped. We took to dirtying our faces and kept all our clothes on, including our gloves, even in warm weather.

Bathing made us stand out in other ways, and one of those ways was we smelled different to the vampires, when we finally found some.

In our time, the vampires were learning what a blood-altered human smelled like, but here we were different because we didn't stink. It was an odd way to attract our prey, but we didn't argue with the results.

Our first few run-ins with 'Pires – solitary and clans – were successful. Although many things weren't working as we'd expected, we persevered and had positive results to show for our efforts. We got to thinking about what we'd do once we'd eradicated the plague, as we called it in this time, about having lives together that didn't involve vampire hunting.

What none of us had taken into account was, before our time, most people didn't believe in vampires.

It's one thing to tell a populace you're fighting an enemy they know and fear – they might assist you or at least get out of your way. But when you're fighting what they consider a figment of your imagination, you don't get support or help – you get persecuted as crazy or evil.

We'd been prepared for the people to be superstitious – we'd planned for it, assuming it would help us win over anyone's help we might need. Unfortunately, we were earning a reputation that far outweighed the dangers of presumed vampires or demons.

"Should the women disguise themselves more?" Jonathan asked, after a particularly unpleasant journey through a small village.

"I'm tempted to say yes," Liam said with a sigh.

"You can't seriously believe we're having problems only because of the three of us," Adrienne protested.

"It's not helping that the people we meet can tell you're women doing what's considered a man's job," David said carefully. "But I agree, I don't believe the three of you are our biggest issue."

"Let them notice us," I said. "Let them know who we are. We're here to save all of humanity, and they're a part of that. Those who realize and understand our purpose will join us, once they realize the virtue of our ways."

"I agree," Hannah said. "We've given up everything else. I refuse to give up being who I am."

"We need to wear the Stars of David hidden, though," Liam said firmly. "More people we meet stare at those than our female team members."

"You mean they hate Jews in this time even more than they hate women," Marcus said under his breath. "They don't hate 'Pires, just people."

"They don't know any better," David said. "We do. That's why we're here."

"Let's hope they learn, then," Marcus replied.

"We'll teach them," I said. "We'll show them the way. We'll gather the few who can stand up to the 'Pires and create our own army."

"Joan of Arc did the same thing," Liam said. "She was burned at the stake for her efforts."

"But she won," I reminded him. "She may have died, but she saved her people."

I wondered how Joan of Arc had felt when she knew she was going to die. Her faith had been strong, so did that mean she went without fear to her death? Or, at the end, was she only alone and afraid, ready to die because everyone who mattered had been lost to her?

I forced my thoughts onto something else.

We went on proudly, at least for a while. Hiding the Stars of David helped, though we were still regarded with the wrong sort of curiosity from most of the populace. However, we met the occasional person who believed us and thanked us for our efforts.

Not that our plan was to tell just anyone what our purpose was. Those few we rescued who weren't more afraid of us than the 'Pire we'd saved them from were given a truthful explanation.

We told any others who asked that we'd been sent by their sovereign to try to stamp out a variety of plague. This worked in many cases. But when you're caught ripping the heads off of supposedly upstanding citizens who just keep odd hours, then you do have some explanations demanded, usually at the point of a sword.

We were equipped to survive against most vampire-based attacks. But we weren't protected from human weapons. And nothing can ever protect you from a mob.

Our first mob was terrifying.

We were caught clearing out a nest of vampires. We couldn't reason with the villagers who were trying to defend their lord and his family. We had to set the vampires' home on fire – not to destroy them but to keep the villagers at bay. They'd kept five horses and we stole them, with two carrying double.

David and Hannah were riding together. In the scramble to escape, his cloak came off and he tossed it over the horse's neck. We rode wildly, feeling more fear of this mob than any vampire.

The villagers gave good chase, though we did manage to outrun them. But not before David took an arrow in the back.

We reached our hiding place and David fell off the horse into Marcus' arms. Hannah leaped off, trying not to cry.

"Can you remove the arrow?" Liam asked Marcus quietly.

Marcus shook his head as he broke off what he could, so Hannah could hold David without harming herself.

"I'll...miss you...my love," David gasped out.

"I'll see you in Heaven, if nowhere else," she whispered, kissing his forehead.

David reached his hand to her face. They were like that for a moment, but only a moment. His hand fell to the ground as his eyes glazed. He looked like Violet to me, only stabbed from behind, not from the front. But the finality of death was the same.

Our first casualty came within a year of arriving. In

a war, I suppose that's a good statistic. In reality, we lost a seventh of our fighting force, and one half of a married couple.

We wrapped David in his cloak and buried him as well as we could, putting a note rolled into an empty vial into his clasped hands. We identified his burial spot with a stone marker. Maybe in time his body would be unearthed, the vial found, and somehow The Order, a thousand years from now, would know their first fallen soldier had died bravely.

At least, we hoped it was bravely. Because we felt more like marauders than heroes. In order to survive, we'd learned to loot 'Pire remains for their money and supplies, just like we'd taken the horses. But what we didn't ask was what this might be doing to our own souls.

Hannah tried to hide her sorrow, but she and David had been together longer than I'd been in The Order. They'd lost everyone to the vampires in our time, everyone but each other.

But this loss was different – deeper, lonelier, more final. We all felt it. Surprising as it was to discover we still had some innocence to lose, but as David's body went into the ground, there was no mistaking the loss.

We finally knew, in our souls, we would die here. Now the only questions were when and would we have completed our mission before the last of us fell?

We found no vampires for another several months. We found other mobs, though. News of us had spread, and it wasn't good news.

The bubonic plague was devastating the population, the Hundred Years War was raging throughout the land, and yet we were targeted as more evil than either of these two horrific calamities. Liam said it was because we were tangible and could be hurt and so gave the people something to react against.

Perhaps.

"Maybe Jonathan was right – they're distrustful because we're women," Hannah suggested, after yet another group had run us off before we'd found if there was a 'Pire in their midst or not. "We dress and act like you men do. Much as I hate to suggest it, maybe that's tipping the mobs off."

"Possible," Liam said. "But doubtful. While this era didn't consider women to have any authority, during these dark times even women could offer last rites to the dying. They should be greeting us with at least a semblance of joy, seeing as we're all clergy and wearing holy symbols."

"You're sure them calling us whores and abominations has nothing to do with our sex?" I could admit it probably wasn't the only reason, but the insults tossed towards Adrienne, Hannah, and me were a little more venomous than those shouted at the men.

"I'm with Liam," Marcus said. "It's too focused to have all these mobs after us simply because we have female warriors in our group."

"Here." Adrienne handed something to me and Hannah.

"What are they?" Hannah asked.

"Leather skullcaps." Adrienne looked embarrassed. "I was going to buy them, but the mob ran us off before

I could."

I examined mine. "There's a hole in the back for our hair."

"I think it makes it more comfortable," Adrienne said.

"Thank you. This should help us hide a little, and they'll be good for battle, too." We had no armor for our heads, and in a fight, even the smallest advantage could turn the tables. The idea of hiding, at least in a small way, didn't seem as outrageous and insulting as it had only a short while ago, either.

Hannah hugged Adrienne. "I'm glad you found these. From a clean shop, too."

"I'm glad we didn't have to buy much gear in this time," Liam said. "Most of what I've seen is even worse than I'd expected."

"I'd glad we were inoculated against the diseases," Jonathan said. "The skullcaps are wonderful, and the rest of us should find our own as soon as possible. I'd also like to find somewhere we can rest and regroup, if only for a short while."

None of us argued with Jonathan's desire. But shelter from the world was hard to find, and not what we'd traveled back in time for anyway.

We were forced farther north, towards the Alps, to escape our newfound reputations as much as to avoid the fighting and the oppressive death. There were times, when we went through a town with more dead in the streets than were still living, that I wondered if the vampires weren't a better option than the Black Death.

But bubonic plague didn't play with its victims, didn't get joy from their pain. The plague we were here to fight was much worse than the Black Death. Though it wasn't spreading as fast we knew it would last far longer.

The vampire plague would outlast the Hundred Years War easily, and it would rage longer and further than the Black Death, too. The vampire plague would prove the adage right – slow and steady would win this race.

Unless we stopped it.

"Maybe the 'Pires don't like the cold," Marcus said. "We should go back south."

"Their influence is here," Jonathan said. "At least, if the standard reactions to our presence are any clue."

"But unless we can find vampires here, influence means nothing." Hannah shook her head. "I agree with Marcus – we should go back."

"We need to go back with a better plan than we've had," I said. "We can't afford to be scattershot anymore."

"David always said there's got to be a pattern," Liam reminded us as we huddled around our campfire. The men had found skullcaps, too, and all of us were wearing them for warmth.

"But we haven't found it in over a year," Jonathan pointed out. "We're finding 'Pires, yes, but they're in random locations."

"If the rumors are true, we should have gone to Romania, not France," Adrienne said. "Perhaps that's what's wrong."

"No, the scientists knew what they were doing," Liam countered. "We're at the point in time when the vampires started to spread and in the general area where the spread started – all the research shows it. We have to find the pattern. Perhaps it's in how they travel."

Marcus shook his head. "Vampires don't wander around, especially the ones of this era. Sunlight is still deadly to them. 'Pires of this day nest."

"So how are they spreading?" Adrienne asked. "How did they leave Romania? And why can't we find the pattern?"

I remembered what Armand had taught me when I'd first joined The Order. "We're not looking in the right places or in the right way. We're not thinking like they think."

Hannah nodded. "We've been here a year, but we're still thinking like 'Pires from our time, not this one. We need to regress our thinking somehow, to match how those of this era think, reason, and react."

"The only nests we've found have been family groups," Adrienne said. "If we look at it like the plague it is, maybe it's something passed through bloodline."

"No," Liam said. "We've found plenty of solitary 'Pires. It's not that."

"Then how is it spreading?" I asked. "We can go for days without seeing another person." At least, another living person. The dead were all around us any time we neared even the smallest populated area.

"Because we're forced to travel through the forests now." Hannah grimaced. "Though even when we were safe traveling on the regular paths we could go a day without coming to a village."

"So, does that mean the vampires are traveling along the regular roads?" Jonathan asked. "And if so, how? I haven't seen an overabundance of coffins being transported, and without that protection, they can only travel at night."

"There are no spare coffins to be had. The dead are in mass graves or rotting in the streets," I pointed out. "In fact, coffins would stand out and give us something to investigate."

"The 'Pires are spreading." Adrienne sighed. "We need to determine how and soon. Before they turn the few who aren't succumbing to the bubonic plague."

"We know they didn't overtake the population," Liam said. "That's not our risk."

Adrienne shook her head. "We've changed things, by coming back in time. The history books you studied never mentioned a small group of people accused of being demons roaming the French countryside, but those history books won't be written for hundreds of years. By coming to the past we've changed it. We don't know what we've done, not truly."

An animal howled in the distance. It was a lonely sound, especially so because no other responded. A shudder went down my spine. I looked at the five others with me. We were all we had here. Losing David had been bad enough. I didn't want to lose any of the others.

Marcus took my hand and squeezed it gently. "We'll figure it out. Don't worry."

I nodded as the others offered reassurance I wasn't sure any of us believed. The animal howled again, alone in the endless night.

Another thing we hadn't foreseen in the far future was that the vampire race's fatal weakness to gold was built over time. By the twenty-fourth century it was a certain weapon. In this time, not as effective by far.

Fortunately, the Nightsticks still worked well for killing vampires. However, we'd been trained to expect just carrying a Nightstick would create real vulnerability in any 'Pire, and this was no longer so. The stunning power still worked in the Middle Ages, but only at close range, and less effectively if the vampire was strong.

This lesson was confirmed when we lost Adrienne. She'd gone scouting alone. When she didn't return as scheduled, the rest of us went after her. We found her in a field, crucified and drained of all blood.

We could tell from the footprints there had been many around her. They'd taken her Nightsticks and the rest of her gear, including her horse, but left her cloak alone.

"How did they drink her?" Marcus asked. "Our blood is poison to them."

"They didn't have to drink her to drain her." Liam pointed to the wet earth around the bottom of the crucifix.

"But her wards and charms," Jonathan protested. "They should have helped her. The 'Pires shouldn't have been able to touch her."

Liam and I examined Adrienne's body. "They sliced open her feet." I felt bile in my mouth as I said this. "They must have watched her blood drain, watched her die."

"Why?" Marcus asked. "I've never seen a 'Pire in this time desecrate a body in this way."

"It's a message," Hannah answered. "They know about us now and they'll fight back differently than they have."

"We're going after them." I wasn't going to wait around for them to come to us. I couldn't allow them to do this to Hannah, to the others...to Marcus.

The others agreed and we followed the tracks to a secluded chateau. No lights burning, but we didn't assume the inhabitants were asleep.

We raided the chateau and found a clan of twenty vampires – they looked like a group of families, probably the chateau's owners and their servants.

They were trying to determine what Adrienne's gear was, some of them playing with the metal vials of holy water. They were avoiding her Nightsticks, but didn't seem bothered much by them. Two wore her jewelry, and some were fingering Adrienne's gold, gold that had been blessed by all of us. The 'Pires weren't affected at all.

We attacked, and two tried to fight back using the Nightsticks. It took a few minutes, but their hands began to burn away and we were able to wrest the weapons back with ease.

They didn't fight in an organized fashion, and though the eldest male seemed to be the leader, he wasn't much of one. "Keep him alive," I called to Liam, just before he dealt a killing blow.

"Why?"

"I want to ask a question."

Liam shrugged but did as I'd asked. He held the

'Pire with a stake at his heart as the rest of us dispatched the remaining clan members. The 'Pire seemed unperturbed.

"Who made you?" I asked as the last of this clan were beheaded and their bodies put onto a pyre.

He shook his head, as if he hadn't understood me. I'd spoken in French, but we were close to the Alps, so I tried Italian. He looked confused. I tried German.

"I will not say," he replied.

"How long have you been made?"

"I was there in the first and will be there in the last."

"Why did you doom your family to this fate? You turned them into demons, abominations in the eyes of God."

He smiled. "Eternal life is not doom."

"None of them will now have eternal life. Nor will you."

He laughed. "Nor will *you*. You are the abomination. Your blood and your body, they are not of this world. We died so that we could be resurrected, to live forever. You are the demons. We killed your sister demon and crucified her according to the laws. We will be rewarded, in this world and the next."

"What do you call yourselves?"

"We are those who live by night."

"Vampires?"

The 'Pire shook his head. "We are not Romanian."

"What are you?"

He smiled wider. "We are your death. We know of you, and we will wipe you abominations off the face of the Earth."

"I've heard enough," Liam snarled. He ripped the

vampire's head off. We tossed his remains onto the rest and watched them burn.

"Is he right?" I asked Hannah as we reclaimed all of Adrienne's gear. "Are we the abominations?"

"No." She put her hand on my shoulder. "Remember the future, the world we come from. The vampires are the enemy, the vicious, bloodthirsty demons who destroyed our lives and our world. Just because the 'Pires of this time are less organized or trained doesn't make them holy."

We waited until the vampires were nothing but ash, then returned to bury Adrienne.

As with David, we wrapped Adrienne in her cloak and buried her, with her charms and another message put into another empty holy water vial, again telling The Order how their warrior had died.

However, we were shaken in ways we hadn't been before. By Adrienne's death, yes, but more by the fact we weren't as strong as we'd thought. We'd known our weapons weren't working as well as they had in our own time, but they were much less effective here than we'd realized until now.

Worse than this, our faith was shaken. While we all tried to discredit what the vampire had said, it was impossible to ignore. And now there were only five of us left against a vampire population that knew what we were here to do.

We continued on, but the 'Pires were on the offensive now. We no longer had the element of surprise, and many times were attacked when we thought ourselves safe. They killed the horses, too, which slowed us down, both in terms of attack and retreat.

Interestingly, our holy symbols had more effect after Adrienne's death. We had no idea why, and we'd still not found the pattern that would help us identify and find their source, but even a small help was better than none.

But small helps aren't much good in a war where one side outnumbers the other by thousands.

At first we questioned every 'Pire we could, before we killed them, but either they knew nothing of what we asked, refused to answer, or said as the other 'Pire had – that we were the abominations, the demons, and they were holy.

Soon we stopped questioning.

One by one, they cut us down. Hannah, Jonathan and Liam each fell during separate fights with vampire clans. Each body was buried as we had David's and Adrienne's. And with each body interred, more of our hope was buried as well.

"Maybe we should...forget this mission," Marcus said as we finished our prayers for Liam's soul.

I stared at the grave. "Liam died in the future, was saved and resurrected, and died again now. Each death was because of the vampires, the plague from this time that grew unchecked for centuries. If we can succeed, stop the plague here, he won't die in the future." Neither would Violet, or David, Hannah, or any of the others. We'd all be alive in the future, if we were successful here in the past.

Marcus took my hand. "But there are only two of

us now." He pulled me to him and held me. "I can't lose you. I couldn't go on alone here without you."

"You could."

"No. *You* could. You've always been the bravest, the strongest of us. I would die here without you to give me a reason to go on."

I leaned against his chest. "Then we'll have to ensure we survive."

He sighed. "I want you to at least consider that we give up this quest. I love you, and I want to live with you, in safety."

"I love you too." I considered Marcus' suggestion as we held each other. Would it be so wrong if we stopped, maybe only for a little while, and just allowed ourselves to actually live?

Marcus knew my resolve was weakening. He started speaking of a future where we would have children, live our lives somewhere safe, where the plague hadn't come. His dream sounded worthy of consideration.

We wandered further north, not really looking for vampires now. Instead, we were looking for somewhere safe to live. I thought of all the vampire homes we'd left behind – if we'd stayed, if we'd stopped and made one of them our base, maybe the others would still be alive and with us.

If we'd stayed – at one of those homes or in our own time – maybe we'd have been safe.

But it hadn't been safe in our own time, and safety wasn't something we'd come to the far past for. I'd never known the luxury of safety.

Marcus was offering safety, but I knew it was a dream, an illusion. We would never be safe. Not as long as the vampire plague existed.

We tried. We truly did.

I removed my cloak, wore a dress and an appropriate woman's head covering, hid my weapons, with the hope of blending in. Marcus didn't have to hide as much, but we both used our cloaks as carrying bags.

Our attempts didn't matter.

We thought to find a village and join it, move into a home none had a claim on any more because the Black Death had killed all potential claimants. But every village we came across ran us off. The insults varied, but the results were always the same.

"Your plan for us to settle down and stop vampire hunting doesn't seem to be working," I said as we trudged away from another place that didn't want us, the shouts and screams of "God doesn't want you here," ringing in our ears.

"Maybe we need to choose a place where all the villagers are dead."

"No. Then we'll be accused of killing them all, should anyone else happen by."

Marcus sighed. "Most likely true." He put his arm around my shoulders and hugged me. "It'll work out."

"Not if we want to live with other people, apparently. They don't like us much, do they? I don't think we resemble any demons from the Bible, but you'd never know."

Marcus was quiet.

"What are you thinking?"

"Maybe God *doesn't* want us here. Maybe we weren't supposed to come back."

"We're doing God's work," I said firmly, even as I admitted to myself that this was a strong possibility. "No religious text lists vampires as agents of good or of God. If we question our faith, our faith weakens."

Marcus chuckled morosely. "I don't have faith in much anymore. Other than you." He hugged me again. "I know if you believe us to be doing right, then we're doing right."

I didn't tell him that I'd stopped wondering if we were doing right months ago. Like Marcus, I couldn't go on if I rejected my purpose. So I continued to embrace it, as I wondered if we could ever truly find safety, or if the mere hope of it was asking for more than we deserved.

We weren't able to find safety. We were, however, able to find vampires.

There was a pattern, just as David had said there would be. I wasn't sure I could see the entire picture, but certain commonalities were appearing to us.

The clans tended to be in more desolate areas, almost always family groups, or tiny communities. The solitary 'Pires were usually in the larger towns. There were exceptions, but by now, we'd accumulated enough kills to feel confident we were reading these patterns correctly.

The town 'Pires had thralls. The family groups

didn't. The families appeared to feed from each other and animals, but not so the town vampires. They had thralls as well as many dead. But with the Black Death still raging, no one looked too closely at the dead. No one but us.

It became easy to spot those a vampire had drained for food – they looked so much better in death than the victims of the bubonic plague.

In some few areas we were asked to give the last rites to the dying and to pray over the bodies of the dead. Our reputations as being evil or dangerous preceded us too often for this to be a common occurrence. We were blamed for the Black Death more frequently than we were hailed as clergy who could give a dying soul peace.

"Someone's telling them about us," Marcus said in frustration after we were run out of yet another town, a town with no vampires in it. "And they're traveling faster than we are."

"Maybe they have telepathy. We know the maker has control over his thralls, and, to a lesser degree, over the vampires he creates. Maybe that's how they're communicating."

"Maybe." Marcus frowned. "That was true in our time. But things are different with the 'Pires of this era."

"The sooner we can determine how they know about us, the sooner we can find the source."

Marcus put his arm around my shoulders. "And the sooner we can find where we want to spend the rest of our lives."

I managed a smile. But I knew where we were spending the remainder of our lives, and want no longer had anything to do with it.

I soon gave up the disguise and again went attired ready for battle. So did Marcus. It changed nothing in how people reacted to us, but we were better able to escape or fight.

We wandered, looking for someplace, anyplace, that would accept us as much as for 'Pires. It was far easier to find the 'Pires than safety or even the mildest of welcomes.

We were still forced off the main roads for most of our traveling. This made finding solitary vampires somewhat easier because either we looked like prey to them or they thought to take us where no regular person would see.

We were deep in a wooded area. The foliage was so dense no sunlight reached the ground. A good place for vampires, just as the last several small forests had been.

The vampire attacked suddenly and swiftly, but Marcus and I were prepared. We fought back-to-back, giving the 'Pire no openings. We ripped the head off, set it on fire, and looted the body.

"This one wasn't too bright," Marcus said as he handed me the small amount of valuables he'd found. "Weak, too. He shouldn't have tried to take us both at once."

The head burned away as we finished and lit the body on fire. I looked around. "Why did this 'Pire attack? He wasn't trying to feed or turn us." I looked at the necklace Marcus had removed from the vampire's neck – a thin leather cord held a wooden Cross of Christ.

"Maybe he thought he'd be a hero and impress the rest of his clan."

No sooner were the words out of his mouth, than we heard the unmistakable sound of a mob approaching.

"There!" a voice shouted. "Just as they said! The killers have murdered Brother Alfonse, defiled his body, and robbed him."

Marcus took my hand and we ran.

We ran through the woods, the villagers after us. Fear is a wonderful motivator and even though we were tired, we didn't slow down.

"There," Marcus gasped as we breached the trees to see a little homestead. "A horse!"

She was a smallish mare, older, and didn't look capable of carrying one person too far, let alone two for any distance.

Marcus ran to her anyway. He hugged me tightly and kissed me deeply. "Ride."

"I can't leave you here!"

He stroked my face, as the sounds of the mob drew nearer. "You can and you will. You're stronger than me, stronger than all of us. And I can face death if I know you're safe."

"Let me fight with you, then. We'll face the mob together."

"No." Conviction I hadn't heard since we'd come

back in time was in his voice. "I've always known that you were the key to our success. Us both dying means our mission and our lives were failures. I don't want that. For me, and the others, you have to survive and go on."

I wanted to protest some more, but I knew he was right. And I couldn't let his sacrifice, or the sacrifice the others had made, be for nothing.

I kissed him again, for far too short a time. Then Marcus picked me up and shoved me onto the horse's back. He slapped her rump and shouted, and the horse ran. I looked back, to see Marcus fighting. All too quickly, the mob surrounded and overpowered him.

I try not to remember the sounds of the mob tearing Marcus apart. But, like so many other memories, it never leaves me.

The mare and I ran on for a few miles. As she tired we reached another wooded area. I headed us into it and we hid.

I waited for nightfall, then snuck back, riding slowly, ready at any moment to make the poor mare run her fastest. But we were unmolested. The villagers had stopped looking for me. Killing Marcus had been enough for them.

They'd defiled his strong body and beautiful face. I didn't care. I still kissed where his sparkling blue eyes had been, and the ragged hole that had once been his mouth.

I wrapped his body in his cloak and gathered what was left of his possessions. Interestingly, the villagers hadn't taken his Nightsticks. Perhaps they believed them instruments of the Devil.

I heaved Marcus' body over the mare's back and

we walked back to the woods. I buried Marcus there, marking his grave as all the others had been.

"Goodbye Marcus, my love. I'll see you in Heaven, if nowhere else."

And it was there that I cried for the first time since that vampire gang in the future had destroyed my life.

I cried for the loss of my love, my family, my innocence, my little sister, and all my friends. I cried because I would never see Marcus' eyes again, I would never talk to anyone who knew and understood me, I would never have a life, only an existence. I cried because I and the others had failed. I cried because God – once my savior – had deserted me again.

The tears flowed for hours. The new day dawned and I still cried. Finally, though, my tears were used up. I lay on Marcus' grave, while I slept and, when my dreams woke me, wondered what to do now.

Light shown through the trees and lit the small sack that held the last vampire's belongings. I dumped them onto the ground. Nothing worth Marcus dying for was in here. Just some few coins and the necklace. I stared at the wooden Cross of Christ for a long time.

The mare and I left Marcus' grave at dawn the next day. I rode her for several days, then let her go near a farm. Every other living thing with me had died horribly; why should she suffer the same fate? She trotted towards the safety of domestication while I stole a handcart – I had what was left of everyone's belongings with me and couldn't carry them alone easily.

This somewhat fair trade made, I headed to whatever fate might hold for me – more alone than I'd ever known someone could be.

I went on with the mission. I had nothing else, after all. Nothing else except for the certainty that the pattern we'd been searching for was almost complete.

My being alone should have meant I was picked off easily. But the opposite was true.

Alone, burdened only with the handcart and supplies, I drew no untoward notice from any people I passed. I killed vampires as I found them, also without too much issue.

The pain of being more effective alone intensified my loneliness. But that pain also honed my focus.

I wasn't looking for stray 'Pires or even clans, but for something more important – the center of the pattern, the point from which the plague radiated. I wore the vampire's necklace, both for remembrance of Marcus and as a talisman to lead me to my goal.

The 'Pire who had attacked us so that the villagers would see us attack him in return had worn a wooden Cross of Christ without issue. The villagers had called him Brother. So at least one vampire had been a man of God before being turned. And at least one vampire had continued to practice as a man of God until Marcus and I had killed him.

The question being begged was simple – how many other men of God had been turned and where had that turning happened? Either the 'Pires had randomly chosen Brother Alfonse or they hadn't. I needed to find out, so I held onto the talisman and looked for its brothers.

It took some time, but the talisman worked.

I reached the Abbey before dusk. The tall, several-storied stone building sat at the top of a small hill. The village buildings were clustered around the Abbey's grounds – it was the center point of this town.

The Abbey looked old and well maintained from the outside. The people cared about it. Or at least, they had.

No one was about – neither human nor animal were apparent to my senses. Not only that, but there were no signs of war, and no signs of the Black Death. Proof the other plague had come here, possibly many years prior.

I pushed at the entry door – it opened without resistance. I drew one of my Nightsticks. I had three others, each nestled in their velvet sheathes, hooked to my belt. They weighed heavily on me, but not as heavily as the loneliness. I didn't allow myself to fear – I couldn't afford the luxury.

The handcart with the rest of my gear I hid in a haystack at the outskirts of this village. I shouldn't have brought the extra two Nightsticks along. I'd never done so before, but they made me feel less alone, as if one of the others, Marcus or Hannah, perhaps, were fighting at my side. I had more than my usual backup with me, that was all. So I told myself. As with loneliness, I couldn't afford the luxury of fear, either.

I listened before I stepped inside but heard nothing. I left the door open to take advantage of the remaining light. Besides, once night came, a closed door wouldn't protect me.

The room was lined with candleholders. Each held a partly burned candle, but none were lit – a bad sign. The grate was cold and empty, and a quick examination showed no fire had been lit for months. For this time of year, a worse sign than the unlit candles.

The room wasn't in disarray, but smelled dusty and dead.

I found a flint and lit the candles, watching for any signs of life or movement. The room was smaller than I'd expected it to be, but this Abbey was more tall than wide. The interior was all dark wood with only a small wooden table and chairs inside. An antechamber, perhaps, used for visitors, with three doors and one stairway leading up.

A single lamp with an unburned candle in it sat on the table. I lit the wick and took the lamp with me.

I checked the doors first. The one to the right led to the large kitchen which accounted for most of the ground level. No one was here and no fresh food was in evidence, either. I smelled only the odor of decay. I did a cursory search – I had a good idea of what was causing the smell.

Nothing. But all this meant was someone had cleaned up. Possibly because they knew I was coming. The thought wasn't comforting, but not a shock, either. Someone had known we were coming for, as near as I could tell, almost as long as we'd been here.

Another door led to the dining hall, also deserted, with no signs of meals taken or interrupted for some time.

The door from the dining room led to the chapel. This Abbey's layout was an odd design, one I hadn't seen before. What this meant I had no way of knowing.

The chapel looked typical – pews, an altar, religious symbols and statuary, a large cross. It was untouched, and the dust layer was thick, thicker than in the other rooms. I sneezed, several times. The dust here was real. The dust elsewhere was something else again, because human ashes never made me sneeze.

The stained-glass windows were intact – one on each side of the room, set to catch the first and last rays of the sun. I stared at the picture of the Resurrection on the western wall and wondered if Jesus had known what plague was to come. A part of me wondered if the vampires were part of God's plan, a way to test humanity – to test me.

Returning to the antechamber, I went to the middle door – this led to the interior yard. There was no one there, but I was able to confirm what the window in the chapel had told me – I was losing the sun.

Unlike most Abbeys, there were no buildings around the yard, merely a low wall, too high for a man to jump easily, but a strong horse or stag probably could. The yard looked serene, with scattered benches, trees that had lost their leaves in preparation for winter, and a small pond.

I went to the pond and performed the cleansing and purification ceremony. I might not get to use this new source of holy water, but without another person to work with I'd found more creative ways to provide backup for myself.

As I finished the ceremony I noted there were no sounds, no animals or insects I could hear. All was

unnaturally still.

My task completed, I returned to the Abbey's interior and checked the last door, the one to the left, by the stairway. It opened into the Abbot's office. Again, nothing disturbed or touched for days, maybe longer. And yet, all the dust everywhere had not made me sneeze – only the dust in the chapel had done so.

I left the office, took a deep breath, and steeled myself for the journey upward. The last rays of the sun slipped away and darkness fell. I was sure now the plague had not only been here, but was still around, waiting, hoping I'd leave or at least make a mistake.

I planned to do neither.

I reached the second story landing and instinct told me no one was here. This floor housed the dormitory. I went cautiously and quietly from room to room, but found no one and nothing amiss. Dust everywhere, but it still didn't make me sneeze.

The only thing I achieved by searching this level was the certainty it was deserted and the minor reassurance it was unlikely someone would be coming upon me from behind.

I went back to the middle of this floor, stood silently, and listened. No insect or animal noises. No sounds at all – except, perhaps, a slight whispering, like silk being drawn gently across skin.

I couldn't tell how many of them were up there, but at least some of this group were on the third level.

By now I was certain a strong clan of vampires had made the Abbey their home. I was also certain they were here, somewhere, waiting for me. Their sense of smell would tell them I was here, but I'd been inside the Abbey long enough they'd have trouble telling if my scent was nearer or not. I could take the time to ensure I was ready.

I loosened my Nightstick holders just enough to allow me to grab a backup but not so their contents would spill out, even if I did a flip. My hair was already tied back, and I pulled my skullcap on. My ponytail hung from the opening in the back of the skullcap and I tucked it inside the back of my vest, in part for camouflage – I was in all black and my hair's reddish-gold hue would stand out – and also to keep my hair from being easily grabbed by my enemies.

I took my infrared goggles out of the small pouch hooked to my belt and put them on. I left the lamp burning – it might confuse them into thinking I was still on the second floor for a few moments. And in these fights, every moment counted.

I fingered the vials of holy water still in my pouch, but left them there. I had a feeling there would be too many for the water to be effective, at least until I could drive them into the courtyard.

Finally I pulled a second Nightstick into my free hand. I wasn't going to be knocking when I reached the top anyway.

I moved upstairs slowly, until I could see the third floor. The end of the stairway led to a door, not a landing. I wondered if this door was locked.

I decided to run the rest of the way, gaining momentum so I could break the door down. If the door was locked, my speed would help me bash through it. If the door was open, then I'd make a more startling entrance.

Not that I was always reckless, but over the past months I'd discovered that sometimes recklessness was the right choice.

I took the stairs two at a time and hit the door with my shoulder. It slammed open and I leapt into the room before the door could swing back. To see dozens of what appeared to be monks wearing brown, hooded robes tied with rope around the waist.

These must have been fighting monks – the room looked like a training area; I'd spent time in a similar room when preparing for my mission. I could have seen all this without my goggles, because there were lit torches along the walls.

I didn't hesitate. My goggles confirmed the story my nose and ears had already told me – none of the bodies in the room gave off enough of a heat reading to be human.

I still seemed to have the element of surprise, which I didn't have time to question. I just spun and grabbed the nearest "monk" with my Nightstick – I got his neck on the first try, clamped the vise, and twisted. His head came off, but not before he managed a shriek.

As the body turned into a puddle of blood and far less savory things, I grabbed the next nearest with my other Nightstick and ripped his head off, too.

Then they were all around me, and as I spun, kicked, hit, and grabbed them with my Nightsticks, I realized that for the first time since my arrival in the past, the Nightsticks were once again working as intended – as they had in the time they'd been created.

While this was excellent news, clearly the entire Abbey had been turned. And with that knowledge came the clarity, the realization, of how the vampires had managed to spread so far and wide and effectively.

The last vampire Marcus and I had killed together had been a monk, a real monk. The vampire plague was being spread through the Church.

Maybe it was because they'd been monks before being turned, but the Nightsticks were stunning these vampires – they moved more slowly than any I'd run across in this time.

Those I couldn't grab with the pincer end of the Nightstick I brained with the rounded end. As the Star of David slammed against them, they dissolved as surely as when I ripped their heads off.

As I fought, I looked for the leader, the vampire who had turned the rest. He was still there, I was sure. The big question was where.

He dropped on me just as I looked up, his face a mask of rage, fangs bared, snarling incoherently. He'd been above me, floating.

He landed, screamed in pain, and ripped off my goggles and skullcap. He was the first vampire of this time to react to my clothing. But he wasn't the first vampire to try this technique, and I was able to drop, spin, and shake him off. As I did, I spotted another vampire staring at me.

He was younger than most of them, maybe in his mid-twenties. He was a bit taller than me, but since I stood less than five and a half feet, this didn't make him a giant. He looked slender under his robe, and his features were rather sharp, but not unattractive. He had a thin moustache that went down the sides of his mouth to meet the beard that ran along his jaw-line.

The leader grabbed me, screaming in pain, and my attention turned back to him. He was a better fighter than the others and dodged my Nightsticks as if we'd fought before and he knew all my feints and parries.

Had we met through the 'Pires he'd created? Vampires had a telepathic link to their maker, it was how a maker controlled his vampires and thralls. Did that link mean they'd given information back to their master?

As I spun, I saw the younger vampire again. He was still staring at me, not fighting, not running, just staring. This wasn't normal, and it unnerved me. The leader called for reinforcements, and I was surrounded.

The young vampire was close to me now, still staring. I couldn't give him my full attention, but out of the corner of my eye I saw him reach for me. I tried to catch him with the Nightstick in my left hand, but he dodged the pincer, grabbed the shaft, and wrenched it from my grip.

The leader laughed, a truly unpleasant sound. "Kill

her. Kill this abomination," he said in Latin as he kicked at me.

"You're the abomination," I said, also in Latin, dodging out of the way. "How many have you made like you?" I thrust my Nightstick towards him and he jumped back.

"Enough." He bared his fangs. "You should have been dead already." He feinted another kick and, as I leaned away from it, he hit my chest. He shouted in pain as I fell back.

"How do you even know I exist?" I regained my footing. The young vampire was nearby, watching us.

"I know because you've killed my children with your weapons." He glared at me. "Through my children you've infected me with your beliefs. You are the last of your kind, and you must be removed from my presence!"

I pulled the wooden Cross of Christ off my neck with my free hand and threw it at him. It hit his forehead and he screamed. The necklace fell to the floor – the vampire had a cross burned into his skin. "She is a demon! Her weapons, her very existence, go against God's will! All of you, destroy her!"

My weapons I'd always expected to be a problem for the 'Pires. But no vampire had ever mentioned my being, my existence, to be an issue. Was it rhetoric or fact? There was only one way to know.

I spun and slammed my free hand against the leader's chest. He shrieked. "Stay back," I shouted. "You cannot touch me and survive because you are the demons...and I am the demon slayer."

For the first time since going back in time, I knew this to be true. I'd found the pattern and its source, and now everything I'd been trained for, everything I'd learned, was once again right.

The leader no longer wanted to touch me. However, this was a training area, and these monks knew how to fight with staffs. The leader grabbed a staff and attacked.

Nightsticks were good weapons, but they didn't have the same kind of maneuverability as a staff did, and they certainly didn't have the reach. I was staff trained, but loathe to let my Nightstick go.

He slammed one end of the staff into my chest, which sent me backwards into some of the vampires around us. I was winded and the 'Pires could have attacked. They should have attacked. But they didn't. Instead they shrieked in fear.

I didn't question. I grabbed one's arm with my Nightstick, using it to pull myself up while I ripped the arm off. The vampire screamed again and I kicked him towards his leader. The staff slammed through the injured 'Pire as I flipped myself forward and to the side.

The vampire dissolved into dust, still screaming, as the leader pulled the staff out and aimed it towards me again, this time swinging it to hit my head.

I leaped forward and down into a somersault, gaining my feet in time to see his staff slam into another vampire's head, taking it off. This vampire certainly had the strength I was used to from my time and rage was clearly making him stronger. Which meant I needed to avoid his blows at all costs.

The 'Pire leader was shouting orders to the others, but they seemed terrified of me. Some muttered about my scent, others about my weapons. Some begged their

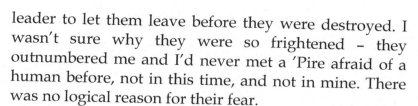

leader to let them leave before they were destroyed. I wasn't sure why they were so frightened – they outnumbered me and I'd never met a 'Pire afraid of a human before, not in this time, and not in mine. There was no logical reason for their fear.

Unless the majority of vampires were afraid because their maker was afraid.

They weren't fighting or attacking me, but they still surrounded us, so limited my options for where to go and what to do. I'd been running on rage, fear and adrenaline. But I'd been fighting for long enough that I was tiring.

The staff came for me again, this time aimed to sweep me off my feet. I jumped but the 'Pire was fast and he flipped the staff up, hitting my side while I was still in the air.

I hit the ground hard and again had the wind knocked out of me. The vampires near me backed away as the leader strode forward, staff raised.

All seemed terrified – except the young vampire. He moved closer, still watching me and only me. His gaze distracted me again, and the leader grabbed me and pulled me up, snarling at the pain his touching me and my clothing caused.

"You die now, abomination," he growled. He looked at the young vampire and shoved me towards him. "Use her weapon. Use it now!"

The young vampire looked straight into my eyes and gave me a small smile as he raised my Nightstick.

The young vampire swung the Nightstick well over my head. I ducked and spun around to see the pinchers connect with the leader's neck.

I watched him wrench his leader's head off.

An unholy shriek came from inside the vampire's headless neck. I'd never heard anything like it, in this time or my own – no vampires had ever made noise after we destroyed them. It took all my training to keep from dropping my Nightstick to cover my ears, but many of the other 'Pires doubled over, screaming.

The sound – a mixture of a crow's shriek, a wolf's howl, and a snake's hiss, amplified a thousand-fold – continued as the young vampire slammed the Nightstick into the leader's body and head, until both dissolved. The unholy sound ceased.

The rest of the clan panicked and started to run. I didn't want them to escape, I wanted them dead. I didn't question the young vampire's motives, I just drew one of my spare Nightsticks and started killing them as fast as I could.

Someone was behind me and a hand reached under my cloak. He pulled the last Nightstick out and wielded two, just as I did. He put his back to mine and fought, almost as well as one of The Order.

A few vampires ripped the long, heavy curtains back and jumped out a window that led to the courtyard. "Stop them! Get them into the pond," I shouted to him in French.

He raced to the window and leaped through. Screams came from down below.

I was still surrounded, but having help, even help I didn't understand, made a huge difference – I was faster, better, more confident. Vampire after vampire fell before me. In less time than I would have guessed, the floor was cleared.

With the curtains open it was easy to see the second stairway at the opposite end of the room. I found my skullcap and goggles, put them back on, and went to it. No door, just a small set of stairs leading up to the bell tower. There were no vampires up here, but I did have a wonderful view of the surrounding landscape.

None of the vampires had escaped over the wall as far as I could tell. Only one body moved down there and it was my helper's. His heat signature looked odd – not human, but not vampiric any more, either.

I didn't have time to ponder this, because we weren't so lucky outside of the Abbey's walls. There were vampires in the town, and from what I saw coming up the hill, the entire populace, like all the monks, had been turned.

I raced downstairs and reached the antechamber as the young vampire came inside. "More are coming."

"I know. Are you willing to help me against them?"

"Willing and able, my saint," he replied. "I am your servant, Alain de Fondeeur."

"Your family were metal casters?" I asked, wondering if I'd translated his name correctly.

He smiled. "Yes. And your weapons were not cast by any in this land. This is one of the ways I know you to be sent from our Lord."

I didn't argue, we didn't have time. "Are there any humans still here?"

He shook his head.

"Then, can you help me to destroy every vampire left?"

He looked confused. "Vampire?"

"What you are, at least, what you were."

"Ah. Yes, I can help destroy the demons, with great willing, my saint. But can none be saved as you saved me?"

I was stunned, but we had little time for me to question what was going on. "Doubtful. If they turn on their kind, maybe. Otherwise, rip their heads off and allow God the final decision."

"As you say, my saint. I am but your disciple."

I considered luring the rest of this vampire hoard into the chapel, to use its very existence as a weapon. But there were enough of them to wait us out and then we'd be truly trapped. "Are we better off staying inside the Abbey or going out to the streets?"

He considered. "The streets. Little of the water is left in the pond and all can leap the courtyard walls. There may be less ways for us to be cornered outside."

I wondered if he was right or if this was some elaborate trap. But I'd asked for his advice. "Outside, then. Good luck."

"God is with us," he said serenely. "I fear nothing now that you are here, my saint."

I didn't share his optimism, but I didn't tell him so. I just prayed he was right.

We left the Abbey and I was relieved to note none of the vampires had reached us yet. They were moving more slowly than I expected. "What's wrong with them?"

"They are held in thrall, my saint. None of them are full demons yet. Most have been turned, just not completed."

"They haven't drunk the vampire's blood?"

"No." A look of revulsion passed over Alain's features. "No, they have not committed that sacrilege. They took orders from our leader. I have killed him, so they have no one to provide direction now."

I had a wild idea, but one worth trying. "Alain, order them to stop."

"I will try, my saint. Hold, all of you!" he shouted.

They slowed even more, but didn't stop. "Try again. Speak in Latin – your leader didn't use French."

He complied, shouting for them to hold in Latin this time. Many of them stopped, and Alain shouted the command in both languages a few more times until all the vampires were standing still, just waiting. "Now what, my saint?"

Now, I had no idea. This was new, completely new. Alain, the village vampires, none of this was within my realm of experience. Years of training and a lifetime of fear and hatred made me want to just kill them all.

Instead I forced myself to examine them. Alain came with me. They were all pale, as Violet had been when she'd been drained. But none of them looked feral, as vampires tended to. Alain wasn't as pale. He looked almost healthy, as if he were alive.

"Why do they understand Latin?" I murmured to myself. Liam had stressed that Latin was reserved for the Church and high nobility only. Alain and the rest of the vampire monks speaking Latin made sense. The peasantry understanding it didn't.

"Because our leader only spoke Latin, my saint. He

155

was not from here. His communication taught them what they needed to know."

"Do you know where he came from?"

"He said Romania, if the words of a demon are to be believed."

The pattern I'd searched so long for was set. The Order's scientists had been right – we'd been sent exactly where and when we should have been. "So, vampires are telepathic."

"I don't understand you, my saint."

"The leader spoke to you in your mind."

"Oh. No. No words. Feelings. Thralls are controlled by words, yes, but more by desire of the master. If the master demon desires something, the thrall will obey."

"The master wanted you to kill me."

Alain smiled at me. "He did. But God sent you to save me, my saint. I was deceived by the demon's words, we all were. We believed his lie that God wanted us to become higher beings, to save the wretched from sickness and horror."

"Did you save anyone?"

"No, my saint. Infected blood makes us ill. Only healthy blood nourishes us."

I looked at the thralls. "None of these are ill."

"No, our village was spared one kind of death, but we embraced another. We have used these thralls for food for many months. Once we drank the master's blood, we became demons, just as he was, so it seemed…right. He wanted us to make more in our image, to spread our kind across the land. He had done so before." Alain looked up at the sky. "He will not do so ever again, my Lord."

"Thanks to you."

Alain looked back to me. "No, my saint. Thanks be to you. What will have us do with the thralls?"

Again my first desire was to say we should destroy them all. But the thralls weren't attacking or defending, merely standing there, waiting to be told what to do. Sheep are not threatening and these vampire thralls were sheep.

But I was a warrior, not a shepherd.

Alain thought I was a saint.

"What do you suggest?" I asked, before my silence went on too long.

"We should see how many have become full demons," he answered without hesitation. "Those who cannot be saved should be killed. Those who can should be spared."

Spared for what? I didn't ask aloud, but the reality of my position came through clearly. If I let them live, they could and probably would do their best to kill me. They would help to spread the vampiric plague throughout the world, until, in my time, it threatened to wipe out humanity for good.

But if I killed them, did that make me any better than they were? I'd spent too long wondering about the safety of my soul to take the risk. And how could I kill Alain? He didn't register as a vampire any more, but he also wasn't human. And he was helping me, willingly. He'd done something I didn't know was possible – he'd overcome the vampiric bloodlust, overcome the demon, to fight against his maker and his clan, to kill them. For

me.

I looked again at the thralls. They were men, women and children, no different from any we'd seen in this time. No different from people in my time. No different from my family. Only they still lived, at least in a sense.

A girl around Violet's age stood nearby. I went to her and touched her hair, waiting for attack. There was none, she just stood there.

"Can thralls ever…act like people do?"

"If the master allows it, my saint, I believe they can. Would you like me to test?"

"Not yet. Have them come with me." I turned and went into the Abbey.

Alain and the thralls followed me. I led them into the chapel. Alain sighed. "It has been so long since I have been allowed in this place, my saint." He looked peaceful and filled with joy. "I thank you for saving my soul, and for giving me this moment."

Most of the thralls looked the same as Alain, though some seemed uncomfortable.

"We'll come back in here later." If any of us, them or me, had a later. I'd made my decision.

I led them all to the Abbey's interior yard. "We wait for sunrise. If any are truly not vampires, or demons, they won't be harmed by the sun's light."

The vastness of my mission spread before me and, for the first time since David had died, I had hope. I looked at Alain. For the first time since Marcus had died I no longer felt lonely. "You should stay in the Abbey, though."

Alain shook his head. "You are with me now, my saint. The sun's light will no longer harm me."

"You can't know that."

"I do know it. The others were willing to follow the demon, but once I tasted his blood I knew I had committed a terrible crime against God. Every day I prayed for the strength to break away. Every night I prayed someone would come to help me, even if it was to kill me before I took the life of an innocent in the way the demon wanted."

"How long?"

"Time is different now. Months, certainly. I had almost given up hope." He took my hand. "And then you arrived, my saint. I knew from your scent, your dress, your weapons, that you were not a regular person, but that you were also not a demon. I saw you slay one of my brother monks and knew God had sent you to save our souls."

"We killed them all."

"We did. And if you had killed me, my saint, that would have been a just decision. But you did not, and God gave me the strength to help you, to destroy the demon. I know God sent you to me, just as I know I no longer need fear the sun's light."

Alain knelt on one knee, still holding my hand. "I am a monk no longer – I am your disciple. I pledge my life to your service, my saint. Where you go, I will go. Your enemies are mine, your mission is mine, and I will protect your life with my own now and forever."

"I've been alone so long." I didn't mean to speak the words aloud.

Alain smiled. "No longer, my saint. No longer."

He rose and led me to a bench. We sat and he told the thralls to sit as well. Then we told each other about our lives before we'd met while we waited for the sun to rise.

Dawn came, and with it the proof that Alain's belief in God was justified.

He stood as sunlight filled the yard, his head turned to the sky, a look of rapture on his face. "Too long, my saint. For far too long I have not felt the touch of the sun."

I did my best to hide my relief as I checked on the thralls. To my surprise, most were reacting as Alain was – they were smiling and looking at the sky.

Some, however, were not so lucky. The cries of pain started as their flesh began to burn. But they didn't try to run – all the thralls smoldering in the sun stayed where they were.

I took a Nightstick and went to the thrall burning nearest to me – the girl who was Violet's age. I didn't rip her head off or club her with my weapon.

"Ashes to ashes, dust to dust, go with God, your sins are forgiven," I said as I made the sign of the cross and then touched her gently with the Nightstick. "I'll see you in Heaven, if nowhere else."

She looked at me. "Thank you," she said, as she disintegrated.

One by one, I went to each burning thrall and did the same. They all thanked me. And after it was over,

Alain held me and dried my tears.

I am no longer alone.

Any time I question my purpose now, Alain says the same thing. "We have overcome the demons, my saint. We have all passed the harshest test our Lord could send and survived, because of you. You are our savior, and we will never desert you."

Alain considers my protection his highest goal. But it is his company that sustains me, helps me to go on. And his love.

We married a year after we met, a year after he says I saved his soul. I say he saved it himself, but he refuses to believe that. Neither one of us truly understands how he overcame the vampiric control, let alone how the majority of his village managed to do the same, but his faith was strong and perhaps God knew I would need help to continue on. Over time, I have stopped asking why or how and just allowed myself to be thankful.

Alain is aging, but more slowly than a human. Due to all the changes done to me before my journey back in time, I'm aging slowly as well. We're both oddities, and yet, we make the perfect team.

He continues to control the thralls and leads them as our small army against the evil undead. But he still calls himself my disciple and takes his orders from me. We sustain losses, but Alain seems invulnerable. No weapons, including the Nightsticks, work against him. He only needs blood at the full moon and only feeds on animals. Otherwise, he eats as I do. The thralls need blood, but they do his bidding and he never allows them to feed from humans.

He creates new Nightsticks as we need them. Our army wields them without issue and to great effect. We are powerful, and righteous, and I can again believe we will wipe the vampire plague from the world.

But still, I wonder and I worry. The baby in my belly seems fine, but how we could conceive is a mystery Alain says we must leave to God.

I don't share my most important question with Alain – will our child be humanity's savior or its curse? Have I found the cure in Alain and our small army of saved undeads, or have I unintentionally created the cause? And if so, will that mean I am the mother of all vampires to come?

I have written this history several times, closed each one into an empty holy water vial, and hidden them. This is the last copy, the last vial. Hopefully one or more will be found in the future. To ease my conscience, to send my apology to The Order – and to the future.

Some things we cannot change. And some things we may change for the worse. As for me, I have found my true family now, and I will protect them until the day I die.

Christabelle de Fondeeur, Year of our Lord 1512

About the Author

Jemma Chase loves writing about vampires, werewolves, ghosts and ghouls. If it's paranormal, it's her cuppa. She thinks the color black is the best color there is, followed by gray, white, and blood red. The only thing Jemma loves more than the paranormal is chocolate, because every girl's got to have a legal vice.

Reach Jemma

Her author page: Blood and Chocolate -
www.ginikoch.com/jcbookstore.htm
The Blah, Blah, Blah Blog -
http://ginikoch.blogspot.com/
Twitter - @GiniKoch
Facebook - facebook.com/Gini.Koch
Facebook Fan Page: Hairspray & Rock 'n' Roll –
https://www.facebook.com/GiniKochAuthor
Pinterest – http://www.pinterest.com/ginikoch/
The Official Fan Site of the Alien Collective -
http://thealiencollectivevirtualhq.blogspot.com/
E-mail –jemma@ginikoch.com

Gini Koch Writing As...

Anita Ensal
A CUP OF JOE

Anthologies
LOVE AND ROCKETS – *Wanted*
BOONDOCKS FANTASY – *Being Neighborly*
THE BOOK OF EXODI – *The Last Day on Earth*

G.J. Koch
ALEXANDER OUTLAND: SPACE PIRATE

Jemma Chase
THE DISCIPLE AND OTHER STORIES
OF THE PARANORMAL

J.C. Koch
Anthologies
THE MADNESS OF CTHULHU - *Little Lady*
A DARKE PHANTASTIQUE - *Outsiders*
KAIJU RISING: AGE OF MONSTERS -
With Bright Shining Faces

Made in the USA
Coppell, TX
25 March 2021